PRAIRIE FEVER

A Cowboys of the Flint Hills Novel

TESSA LAYNE

Playing doctor has never been so sexy...

Confirmed bachelor Gunnar Hansen, has successfully resisted the matchmaking efforts of Dottie Grace and her posse of granny wannabe's. There's no room in his life for love, or for starting a family of his own. Not when his hands are full running Hansen Stables and heading up the board of Prairie's new medical clinic. But everything turns upside down when the socialite who ditched him at the altar years ago turns out to be Prairie's new doctor.

Four years ago, fresh out of medical school, Suzannah Winslow took a gamble on a sweet-talking cowboy who left her high and dry... and pregnant. With her residency behind her, and an offer to become Prairie's first and only physician, she can finally provide her daughter with stability she's longed for. She has no interest in taking a second chance on a silver-tongued cowboy full of empty promises. Even if his smile still melts her panties.

But Gunnar has other ideas, and when he mounts a full-scale campaign to win back the woman he lost, will little Lula Beth become his unlikely ally or the wedge that drives them apart for good?

Chapter One

Gunnar Hansen cursed silently as the phone in his rear pocket vibrated furiously. He'd lost count of how many times it had gone off in the last thirty minutes. Too many damn times. Shaking his head, he turned back to the new mare he'd spent the afternoon training.

As far as he was concerned, this day could go to hell.

The phone rang again. "What?" he barked, not bothering to check the ID. It didn't matter who it was, anyone bothering to call was bound to be pissed.

The mare tensed, flicking her ears, and he patted her neck absently as Dottie Grace's voice crackled through the speaker. "Calm down, calm down. Take a big ole breath and untwist your britches, for a second, will you?"

Gunnar took a steadying breath. It wouldn't do to piss her off more than he already had. She'd covered for him more than enough over the last few months. "I know, I know. I'm sorry. Day got shot to hell when the farrier's truck broke down outside of Ottawa. I swear I'll be there as soon as I can."

Dottie chuckled. "It's always something with you lately, Gunnar. Makes me think you're not interested in being head of the clinic board."

"No, no." Gunnar shook his head. "That's not it at all." Okay, maybe it was a little bit, but he wasn't about to shirk his family responsibility. After all, he was the oldest Hansen, and resigning from the board would break his cousin Maddie's heart. With no family and no wife, he was the logical choice, the *only* choice. Everyone else was caught up in Prairie's mini baby boom. Maddie and his sister, Hope, were both pregnant, and his little brother was happily settled in Oklahoma, also with a new baby. He grimaced inwardly. Being alone at thirty-two hadn't been his choice, but after what happened last time, he wasn't about to go down the marriage and baby road again. No, sirree. He'd grow old running Hansen Stables and the Warren G. Hansen Memorial Clinic Board, and that would be that. Let him play the fun uncle to his nieces and nephews.

Gunnar ran a hand through his sweat-slicked hair, fighting exhaustion. His plate might be overfull, but he'd manage. "I'm happy to run the board, Dottie. I wouldn't let you down like that. I'm sorry it's been crazy lately."

Dottie harrumphed. "And don't you dare come runnin' in, stinking to high heaven like you did at the last board meeting. We know you're busy, but for God's sake, we don't want to scare off Dr. Winslow. She only just got here. She's a pretty thing, too," Dottie said after a pause.

"Oh no," Gunnar protested, clenching his jaw. "You and your posse of granny wannabes need to let up. Not interested. Especially when Dr. Winslow reports to the head of the board."

Dottie clucked. "We both know small towns work

differently. Besides you have an entire board to keep you in check."

"And *you* know there are plenty of babies in this town on the way already. Without me." He emphasized the last two words in case Dottie misunderstood. Not that she would. The woman didn't miss a thing.

"Can you be here in an hour? I'm not waiting any longer to put out the pies."

"I'll be there as soon as I can."

It took the better part of an hour to get Sugar groomed and settled, adding to Gunnar's already sour mood. He couldn't help that the mare was naturally high-strung, and still skittish of her new surroundings. All he could do was stay calm and give her as much time as she needed to settle. If the board couldn't understand that, then fuck 'em. He wasn't going to traumatize a good animal for a party. If he had to make his apologies to the good doctor after the fact, then he'd do that. She was going to have to learn how country time worked anyway.

As he cleaned up, Gunnar's thoughts turned to Dottie's remarks. So the new Dr. Winslow was a looker? She'd have no shortage of would-be boyfriends, then. In fact, he grinned tightly, if she fell in love with a local and got married, then she'd certainly stay beyond her five-year commitment. All the better for the town's investment. Let someone pursue her, so long as it wasn't him. Until Hansen Stables financial picture was more secure, he had his hands full at home.

On the dresser, Gunnar's phone vibrated. He grabbed it, glancing down.

Ma: *Are you coming?!? Dessert is almost over.*

Shit.

G: *Tell Dottie I'm on my way... I swear.*
Ma: *The new Dr. is very nice :)*

Great. Not her too. She wanted grandbabies so desperately. Especially now that his father was slowing down. It didn't matter that one granddaughter was only a few hours away, or that Hope was expecting. It was like some kind of a contest with the older women in town. "She who has the most grandchildren wins," he muttered, jamming the phone in his back pocket and slamming the door behind him.

The tires squealed as they made contact with the pavement. If he pushed his speed, he could get to the diner in under fifteen minutes. As long as he didn't get stuck behind a tractor. This time of year, anything was possible. He sped along the main road leading to Prairie's Main Street, drumming his fingers on the steering wheel and rehearsing his apology speech to the new doctor. Now that he was on his way, guilt settled in his belly. He'd dodged Dottie's questions for months about why he'd blown off the search process for a town doctor. Why he'd been uninterested from the get-go, and willing to let the board do whatever they saw fit. He trusted them implicitly – at least that had been his line with Dottie, who gave him the stink-eye every time he waved her off, saying it was more important for the board to have ownership of the process.

What a load of horse shit.

Dottie knew it too, but she'd never figured out why. He'd played those cards too close to the vest. The only one in town who knew the truth was his cousin, Parker, who'd kindly kept his mouth shut about the real reason Gunnar had taken a hands-off approach to the whole thing.

~

4 1/2 Years Earlier

Parker checked his watch impatiently. "Dude. Colton Kincaid's going to ride at eight. If we don't leave soon, we're going to miss him. The Strip's already at a standstill."

"Just a few more minutes," Gunnar growled. "Something must have happened."

Parker smirked, arching a brow. "I think your balls have been busted."

"Fuck you," he snapped. "Suzannah's not that type of woman."

The look on Parker's face said otherwise. "I think you left your thinking brain back in Prairie. C'mon. Who falls in love and gets married this fast?" Parker opened his hands. "Sure, we've all been in instalove at one point or another, but even *I* know you don't know this chick well enough to marry her."

"She's not a chick," Gunnar bit out, looking to his brother for help. Axel just shrugged, giving him a look that said *"Sorry, dude."* Fuck him. Fuck *them*. They didn't understand. How could he even *begin* to explain what the last three days had been like? He could barely articulate it himself, but he *knew*. He knew with the deepest part of himself that Suzannah Marie Harper was the woman he was destined to spend his life with. Fate had brought them together. He was certain of it. And while it might seem irrational to onlookers, heck – his parents would shit their pants when he returned home to Prairie and announced he'd gotten married in Vegas – this was the sanest decision he'd ever made.

An hour and three drive-through weddings later, still

no Suzannah. Parker shook his head grimly. "I'm outta here. Wait if you want, but I'm not gonna miss Colton's big ride. Not with the championship on the line." Parker tilted his chin. "Axe, what are you doing?"

Gunnar's stomach dropped to his boot heels.

Axel shot him a guilty look. "I'm sorry, man."

Pain knifed through Gunnar. His chest burned and he scrubbed a hand across his jaw, letting out a ragged breath. "Go." He waved his brother off. "I'm gonna wait a bit longer."

The look in Axel's eyes shot straight through him. He was a fucking idiot. He'd been played. And Axel was too nice to point it out. *She couldn't have played him.* This felt all wrong. "You sure?" Axel asked. "If you want me to stay…" his voice trailed off.

He shook his head once, stomach hollow. He'd face his humiliation alone. "I'll be all right." Somehow.

"Do we need to set a rendezvous point?"

Gunnar barked out a laugh. "If she shows, the first place we'll go is the phone store so I can text your sorry disbelieving ass a photo."

"And if she doesn't?"

The words gored him like a raging rodeo bull. "Then you can find me in the hotel bar."

Axel gave him a crooked smile and grabbed his shoulder. "I'll look for the text."

He wouldn't. Axel knew what he wasn't ready to admit yet. She wasn't coming.

Lights flashed in the rear-view, and the blip of the

police siren sounded. Motherfucker. Gunnar glanced down at his speedometer as he hit the brakes. This day could just go to hell. Hopefully Prairie's police chief, Weston Tucker, had tagged him and not one of the recruits. Weston understood how Dottie could be when she got a bee in her bonnet. He also knew about the welcome party for the new doctor. Heck, he'd probably stopped in himself.

Gunnar rolled to a stop on the shoulder, giving a sigh of relief when he saw Weston step out of the SUV and adjust his aviators. He rolled down the window and nodded a greeting. "Sorry, man. My brain was elsewhere. Dottie's fit to be tied that I've missed most of the welcome party for Dr. Winslow."

Weston adjusted his stance and crossed his arms, shaking his head. "Do you know how fast you were going?"

"Shit, I don't know. Fifty? I've been running late all day."

Weston shook his head slowly. "Wanna guess again?"

He couldn't have been going *that* fast. Weston was a stickler for drivers observing the speed limit. Everyone knew it, too. "Sixty?"

"Eighty-two."

"I can explain," Gunnar started. Weston seriously wouldn't give him a ticket, would he? Heck, they'd just sold the guy a horse he was crazy about.

Weston cut him off. "I can't let eighty-two in a forty-five slide. At that speed, you're a danger to yourself and everyone else on the road." He pulled out a small clipboard.

Gunnar dropped his head back against the seat. "Dottie's gonna kill me."

"Better a tongue lashing than vehicular homicide."

He knew better than to argue. Weston was a hard-ass. And that's what made him a great police chief. It didn't matter how much he liked you, he had no problem giving you a ticket when you deserved one.

The phone buzzed from its place on the console. Who was it this time? Dottie? His mom? Maddie? His sister? A weight settled across his chest. He hated letting them down, and right now it felt like that's all he'd done lately. He held out his hand for the ticket. "Can I go now?"

Weston signed the ticket with a flourish. "I dropped it to thirty over. Still a hefty fine, but you won't get your license yanked. Slow the fuck down, okay?"

Gunner nodded, clamping down on the smart-ass retort on the tip of his tongue. He fell in behind Weston's SUV and drove the remaining distance to Main Street doing five under. The parking lot was virtually empty when he pulled in. Not a good sign. Worse, he didn't recognize any of the vehicles. His parents must have hit Gino's Trattoria for a late dinner. Maybe he could join them after he'd accepted his tongue-lashing and drown his sorrows in a bowl of spumoni. Shutting the door with too much force, he rolled back his shoulders, jammed on his hat, and rounded the corner to the entrance. Normally a welcome sound, the bells jangled too brightly, announcing his arrival.

Dottie's head snapped up from her usual position behind the counter. The fire in her eye, combined with the pinch at her mouth, told him everything.

Where in tarnation have you been?

I will never let you hear the end of this.

She jerked her chin in the direction of a youngish woman talking quietly with a couple of women he recognized as part of the granny brigade.

Gunnar paused, taking in the scene. Dottie was right, even from behind, he could tell the woman was a looker. Five-ten by his estimate, lush curves that tugged at his memory. Suzannah had been curvy as sin. A real-life Jessica Rabbit, but blonde. A memory seared him. The two of them, naked, standing in front of a mirror, one hand splayed across her hips, the other nestled in a thatch of golden curls, caressing her sex.

His body went tight. Was the memory of her bound to haunt him at every turn today? On second glance, the woman in front of him was too prim, wearing dark slacks and a light sweater, golden hair pulled tight into a bun at the nape of her neck. Although her ass was damned near perfect, he preferred someone a little less buttoned-up. A little more passionate and fluid. A little more like how he remembered Suzannah – a woman in touch with her sensuality. From behind, this woman looked like she had a stick up her ass, which would make it that much easier to maintain a strictly professional relationship, well-intentioned grannies or not.

"Sorry to keep you waiting," he called, weaving through the tables to where the women stood.

Three heads turned his direction, but the floor tilted as he locked eyes with Prairie's newest resident. Heat flooded his body and his boots stuck to the floor as the greeting died on his lips. Gunnar's stomach dropped like a stone. He flushed hot, then lost feeling in his limbs as white hot anger replaced shock. For a split second, his head exploded – all the unspoken words, all the hurt, swirling with the fury of an F-5 tornado.

As if in slow motion, her eyes sparkled, then widened, and went blank. At the same time, the color drained from her face, smile freezing then vanishing.

So.

Suzannah Marie Harper recognized him too.

Chapter Two

_N_o. Way.

No *fucking* way. Suzannah froze, unable to believe what her eyes were telling her. *This* was head-of-the-board Gunnar? She'd expected someone in their fifties, not *him*. Not the man who stole her heart, then broke her.

And good lord... somehow, in the time that had passed, he looked better than ever. His face was more chiseled, more defined. The last of his boyish softness had disappeared, now replaced with hard man. His hair was shorter now, no longer the long ponytail he'd sported in Vegas that gave him the appearance of being a Viking warrior, especially with his shirt off. She missed the long hair. He was bigger than she remembered, broader, muscles more defined, stretching the fabric of both his shirt and his jeans. Her pulse tripped, and her body betrayed her. This was the man who abandoned her at the altar. She should be cool, indifferent, not unable to tear her eyes away, mouth watering over the thought of him naked.

Why hadn't she thought to ask more about him in her interview? The name had set off a warning bell when she'd applied, but she'd also been a finalist for a similar program in North Dakota, where she'd met three Gunnars – all wizened old men descended from Swedish pioneers. In the end, she'd accepted the offer in Prairie so she could be closer to Kansas City, and her best friends. Her only support system for the last four-and-a-half years. The idea of being more than a few hours away had been unbearable. And not just for her. Lulah adored her aunties.

Gunnar dropped his hand, blue eyes like a glacier. "Hello, Dr. *Winslow.*" Sarcasm dripped from his voice.

Beside her, Gloria McPherson gasped quietly. Fine. She deserved that. She'd planned to explain a few things at the altar, but she hadn't gotten the chance. They'd been too starry-eyed, high on hormones, champagne, and willing to throw caution to the wind. They'd bared their souls to each other, the names of their first pets, the foods they hated growing up, even the names they imagined for their children. Yet, she'd been too scared to disclose her last name – her father's persona had a way of scaring people off.

Her mouth went dry. She needed to say something. The women were looking at her, aghast. Digging deep for a small smile, she extended her hand. "Hello, Gunnar. Nice to see you again." She could barely hear her voice over the pounding in her ears.

He glared, refusing to accept her hand. A flash of anger whipped through Suzannah. Why did he look so furious? *He* was the one who ditched her. Refused to answer her frantic phone calls and texts, and was long gone when she finally made it to the little chapel where they'd planned to take the plunge. *He* was the one who'd smashed her heart to smithereens and left her to deal with the fallout.

"Gunnar Hansen," Dottie boomed. "Where in tarnation are your manners? The least you can do is offer Dr.

Winslow a chair and a piece of pie. Your mama raised you better than that."

Suzannah bit back a smile. She liked Dottie Grace more and more. Gunnar's eyes narrowed, but she held his gaze, unflinching. She'd been through hell and back since they'd kissed goodbye on the Strip, and it was going to take a lot more than an ice-cold glare to make her squirm. She'd dealt with doctors who were far worse. Heck, her father was far worse.

"I'll grab the pie," Gloria said in a rush, clearly ill at ease.

It would be rude to leave without a piece of pie, but she refused to be the target of Gunnar's ire a second longer. Flashing him a bland smile, the kind she'd been taught from day one in sixth-grade cotillion, she pulled out the chair closest to her and offered it with a sweep of her hand. "Have a chair?"

He nodded curtly and moved toward her. As he sat, Suzannah caught a whiff of his cologne, a heady combination of bergamot and cedar. Her chest clutched in recognition, the force of it snatching her breath. Once upon a time, she'd wrapped herself in that scent, luxuriated in it. And in moments of weakness in the dark days that followed after their last kiss, she'd haunted the cologne counter at Hall's, letting the scent and the memories wash over her.

She circled the table and dropped into a chair across from him. Better to keep a little distance. Her chest pinched, questions and hurt rising unbidden, ready to tumble out of her mouth the second she let down her guard. But her guard wouldn't come down so easily. Not this time. Not when she had more than herself to worry about.

Gunnar held her gaze, glare gone, but definitely assessing. Suzannah stared right back, heat curling up her chest. Let him look all he liked. Let him realize what he gave up by throwing her away like a piece of trash.

His jaw remained tight, mouth firm. That mouth had done sinful things to her body, the memory of it permanently imprinted on her soul. His fingers, long, strong fingers that had brought her to climax so often she couldn't remember her name, drummed casually on the table, the only outward sign that he might be agitated. He'd been the consummate poker player. At least he *had* been. Could he still bluff a table with nothing but a pair of threes and walk away with the winnings?

Gloria bustled back with thick slices of chocolate cream pie, and paused, eyes darting back and forth between them. "You've met before."

Here it was. The first moment of truth. There was no use denying what was patently obvious. Her mind whirled. More was at stake than just her job. She should resign tonight. Go back to Kansas City and try to find a job in a family practice, resign herself to a lifetime of medical school debt. Her girlfriends would be thrilled to have her back in town. Or maybe there was another rural community far, far away from Prairie that had a similar program for paying off student-loan debt in exchange for years of service. Either way, it was clear coming to Prairie had been a huge mistake.

She arched a brow at Gunnar, daring him to speak. Her heart gave a curious little jump when the muscle at his temple twitched. Her mouth turned up as she nodded once, slowly. "Yes. Yes, we have."

Gloria clucked, shaking her head. "I'm gonna help Dottie shut things down. Holler if you need a refill." She scurried back to the kitchen.

Any other day, the cream pie would have tasted heavenly. Today? The crust felt like sandpaper, and only the barest recognition of chocolate hit her brain. The longer they sat, the more the silence ate at her. Four-and-a-half years and the best he could do was give her the silent treatment?

Anger sparked to life deep in her belly. If that was how he wanted to play it, fine. Let him sit there, all big and broad, blue plaid shirt pulling tight across his chest, showing the faintest hint of the chiseled muscles beneath. She'd already explained herself, repeatedly. In frantic, teary voicemails and texts. He'd never responded, not once. Better she learned before she'd said *I Do*, that he couldn't handle even the slightest emergency. Contrary to his silver-tongued promises, he wasn't cut out to be a doctor's husband.

Suzannah forced herself to chew slowly, to keep a lid on the anger that threatened to spill out like a volcano. She'd learned a few things from her crazy family, the first being that she who revealed feelings first, lost. The second, she who spoke first, lost. If Gunnar wanted to make this a battle of wills, game on. But this was about more than her, her conscience pricked, and whatever battles she fought, needed to be fought with that in mind.

For now, her questions would have to remain unanswered. Her hurt, buried and re-examined at a later date. She didn't need to reveal her feelings to Gunnar at all. She owed him nothing. Drawing up her courage, she laid down her fork, then dabbed the corners of her mouth with her napkin. Then she placed both hands on the table, pushed back her chair and stood, resolve straightening her spine to an iron rod. Once again, gratitude for her height washed over her. There was power in her stature, and she needed every scrap she could get right now.

"My full name is Suzannah Marie Harper Winslow."

Gunnar's eyes widened a fraction.

"You've probably heard of my father, Orrin Winslow, one of the biggest real estate developers and business investors in the Midwest?" She rarely disclosed that bit of information, preferring to live a more anonymous life, far away from the media attention he enjoyed nearly as much as the money he seemed to create out of thin air. Gunnar started to speak, but she held up her hand. He didn't deserve any other explanation. "There's nothing more to discuss. The board will have my resignation in the morning." Squaring her shoulders, she spun on her heel and marched out of the diner.

Chapter Three

---

*S*tunned.

Fucking stunned.

She acted like he was at fault. Like *he* had wronged her. He'd kept waiting for her to offer some kind of explanation, an excuse, an apology, something, *anything*. And now Dottie was storming over, looking as ruffled as a prairie chicken defending her nest.

"Never in all my years of knowing you, have I seen you behave like an ass," she stormed. "You are *better* than that, Gunnar Hansen."

His chest lurched. He hated disappointing people. His family most of all, and while he might not be related to Dottie Grace, she was family. "You don't understand," he started, then stopped, unsure he was ready to make his confession. Once Dottie learned about what happened in Vegas, everyone would know. Including his parents.

Dottie harrumphed, fisting her hands on her hips. "Then you better make me, sweetie pie, because there will be hell to pay if you've scared away that sweet thing."

"I didn't scare her away," he snapped, burning at the

insinuation that somehow this was his fault. "She resigned on her own."

"*Resigned?*" Dottie's voice rose an octave. "Let me see if I understand this." She waved an arm, getting more worked up by the second. "The board that *you're* in charge of, the board you've *neglected*, searched for *months* for the perfect candidate, and the night before Day One, you blow in here – *late* – wearing an expression that would terrify a demon, and scare her off without saying more than six words to her?" Dottie shook her head vigorously, mouth thinning to a straight line. "You are not leaving here until you've spilled. *Everything.*" She turned and called back to the kitchen. "Gloria, hon, can you bring out the crisis bottle? We have a situation here."

Crisis bottle?

"Since when did you start drinking whiskey?" he choked out, hardly believing his ears.

"When Jamey was helping me with the food truck after the tornado last year, she brought a bottle. Got to where I enjoyed a little nip at the end of a long day."

Jamey Sinclaire and her husband Brodie, worked the hunting lodge not far from where the Hansen property butted up against the Sinclaires'. With red hair and a fiery personality to match, she'd introduced many of Prairie's ladies to her favorite Irish whiskey, a twelve-year Redbreast she termed 'the crisis bottle.' According to his little sister, Jamey's crisis bottle had resolved more than one romantic conflict in town.

Gloria bustled out of the kitchen carrying the bottle and a stack of small juice glasses. She set the bottle down with a *thunk*, then laid out the glasses. She eyed Gunnar with a gleam in her eye as she splashed whiskey into the glasses. "Don't think for a second I'm not going to eavesdrop on this conversation."

Great.

He wasn't sure which was worse, confessing to his mom, or to Dottie and another member of the granny posse. At least Axel wasn't here. That would be much, much worse. He could just hear Axel snickering at the whole situation. Like a good younger brother, Axel never missed an opportunity to needle him, although he'd been surprisingly sympathetic when Suzannah had abandoned him at the altar.

Dottie and Gloria stared at him with an air of hunger. Prairie's older women were like bloodhounds when it came to ferreting out gossip. They could smell a juicy story a mile away.

Stalling, he drained his glass in one swallow, letting the whiskey roll over his tongue and burn his throat. He was going to need another glass *at least*, before he was willing to spill the beans.

"That bad, huh?" said Dottie, raising a brow and giving him a motherly pat on the arm.

Oh shit.

All the shame and bitterness he'd buried, carefully contained in a secret part of his soul, geysered up and shot out of his mouth before he could stop the words.

"She took me for a ride, Dottie. Completely snowed me. Got me to promise her the goddamned moon on a silver chain, and then she stood me up. Left me standing at the altar with Parker and Axel, looking like a damned fool." He slammed back the second shot, returning the glass to the table with a little too much force. The burn of the whiskey didn't begin to come close to the inferno in his veins.

She thought she could quit and march out of here, head held high? Screw that, he meant to fire her. Let her have a taste of the humiliation he'd experienced that night.

Gloria let out a tiny giggle. Dottie chortled.

"There is nothing funny about this," he snapped.

"Of course there is," Dottie shot back. "What in Baby Jesus' name were you *thinking?* Who gets married in Vegas? How long had you known each other? A day? Maybe two? What brain were you thinking with?"

Gloria was now giggling uncontrollably, tears leaking from her eyes. Gunnar shook his head. They had no idea what it had been like, how intense it had been. "Four," he muttered. "Four days." Four perfect days of soul-searing kisses, followed by sharing their deepest secrets, their closely held dreams. It was like Suzannah Harper, Suzannah *Winslow*, had been conjured from his dreams. They were meant for each other. There'd been no choice for either of them, except to marry.

Dottie shook her head, tsking. "If you'd come home from Vegas with a wife you'd known only four days, I'd have slapped you silly."

"It wasn't like that. I could tell you things about Suzannah no one knows." Like the heart-shaped tattoo on her right hip bone. Or that her dog, Misty, had been hit by a car when she was eight. And that she wanted to name a daughter Talulah for her grandmother who she loved more than anything.

"I don't care what you know or don't know about Dr. Winslow," Dottie retorted. "I don't care if she can play the piano with her toes. We're damned well not going to let an excellent physician get away, and a single mother at that, because your penis had a momentary lapse of judgment. She needs us as much as we need her."

Gunnar's hand fisted on the table. "What do you mean?" he asked when he finally found his voice. A wave of jealousy rolled through him with teeth-jarring intensity, as the picture of her, belly distended and heavy with child, shimmered before him. It should have been him. His stomach hollowed at the thought, acid rising in this throat. He'd have happily given her all the children she wanted.

Dottie started to speak, but Gloria nudged her. "Not our story to tell, Dot." She speared him with a look only a mother could give. "It sounds like the two of you have some catching up to do."

Had she married someone else? Had some asshole knocked her up then abandoned her? A flash of fierce possessiveness speared him. Family meant everything to him, and the knowledge that Suzannah was raising a child on her own didn't sit well with him. He might be pissed as hell at her, but he wasn't so much of an asshole that he'd push her out of town when she was raising a child on her own. What if she had nowhere to go?

"Darn tootin'," Dottie agreed. "And don't even *think* of showing your face back here until you've convinced our doctor to stay."

Gunnar nearly turned around three times on the ten-minute walk to where the clinic stood on the edge of town. Across the street from the clinic stood a bungalow, built in the forties, with a wide front porch and stone pillars. The Graces had donated the house to the Warren G. Hansen Memorial Foundation, and Mason Carter, a millionaire friend of his cousin Maddie's husband, had paid for the remodeling.

The lights were on, and two cars stood in the driveway, one with Missouri plates. She had company. The child's father? His stomach lurched at the possibility. That was more than he could face. Instead, he kept walking, blood drumming in his ears. What was he supposed to say? *Hi, I'm sorry I was a d-bag back at the diner. Why did you ditch me?* He paused at the corner. He couldn't do this. Not yet.

Reaching into his back pocket, he grabbed his phone

and scrolled through to Axel. Desperate times called for desperate measures.

Axel picked right up. "'Sup?"

Gunnar took off his hat and wiped an arm across his forehead. "Got a sec?"

"Sure. What's going on?"

He sucked in a breath then forced it out. "You remember Suzannah Harper?"

"Of course." Axe's voice went hard as iron.

"She's here. In Prairie. The board hired her to run the clinic." Gunnar held in a breath as he let the news sink in.

Axel laughed. "You're shitting me."

"Not at all." He held out the phone as Axel continued to laugh uncontrollably. Not exactly the reaction he'd hoped for out of his brother, but the one he probably deserved, given their history.

"Let me get this straight," Axel wheezed while catching his breath. "The chick–"

"She's not a chick," Gunnar growled.

Axel snorted. "The chick you picked up in Vegas, and decided to marry after three days, who then *wisely* didn't show–"

"Hey–" That stung.

"Dude. She could have been an axe murderer. Or a con artist."

"Yeah, well she's a doctor."

"And you're calling me because?"

Gunnar could hear the smirk in his voice. Maybe it was a mistake calling Axel, but who else could he talk to? Who else knew? Parker. But he wasn't ready to face Parker's ribbing. "Well, it's going to be all over town tomorrow that we've met before," he snapped.

Axel grew serious. "Since when did you take the coward's way out? That's not your style, man. Town can't afford to lose her, and you know it. Think about Uncle Warren."

Gunnar shut his eyes, reliving the aftermath of the tornado that had ripped through Prairie just over a year ago. His uncle's body broken and bruised, dying before their eyes because help was too far away. The memory still churned his stomach. Letting out a heavy sigh, he nodded. "You're right."

"Wait. Say that again?"

"I said you're right."

"One more time,"

Gunnar huffed out a dry laugh. "Fuck you, asshole."

"Love you, too, man."

"Give that baby girl of yours a hug and a kiss from Uncle Gunn. See you soon?"

"Fourth of July."

Gunnar ended the call, and slowly walked back down the street, chest tight. Marriage had been good for Axel. It might have been good for him too, if he'd been given the chance. But his lot had been cast – bachelorhood forever. Even if the woman who'd stolen his heart was back in his life. He wouldn't make the same mistake again. But he *would* make things right, and convince her to stay. For Prairie.

He paused at the walk. A swing hung at one end of the porch, and just in front of the screen door, a red tricycle stood, abandoned. What drew him forward though, was the light spilling out from inside, providing a welcome glow in the fading light. Gunnar steeled himself. He could do this, even if the Missouri plates belonged to the dad. He was just here to ensure Dr. Winslow didn't quit and leave the residents of Prairie high and dry. Nothing more. No need to bring up the past. Ask any one of the hundreds of questions that burned in his brain.

Before he could knock, a tiny thing, white blonde hair spilling out in waves from behind a pair of Batman glasses and wearing a homemade cape ran up to the screen and stopped, staring. "Are you a good guy or a bad guy?" she asked, voice high and pipy.

Everything inside Gunnar melted at the sight of her. Was this Suzannah's child? He pushed back the wave of longing at what might have been, and smiled down at her. "That depends." On so, so much. He was pretty certain Suzannah thought he was a bad guy, although for the life of him he couldn't figure out why. *She'd* stood him up.

"Lulah." A voice, not Suzannah's, called sharply from within the house. "Is someone at the door?"

Lulah? His stomach hollowed. Had she named her daughter Talulah after all? His chest pinched in envy. Tiny ran off, bare feet slapping against the hardwood, and seconds later a woman bustled to the door, smile fading when she recognized him.

Gunnar cleared his throat and offered a conciliatory smile. "Iris? It's Iris isn't it?" He remembered her from Vegas, one of Suzannah's best friends.

Her brown eyes snapped fire. "Don't you think you've done enough damage already?"

His head snapped back as if he'd been slapped. "*I've* done enough damage? I'm not the guilty party here. I just want to make sure–" This was an exercise in futility. Arguing with Suzannah's self-appointed gatekeeper would get him nowhere. "Look, can I please talk to her?"

Shooting him another glare, Iris turned and disappeared. Given the look on Iris's face, he wouldn't put it past her to make him wait as long as possible. But he could play this game, too. He'd wait all night if necessary. He wasn't leaving without talking to Suzannah. One minute, two minutes. He retreated to the porch railing, taking a seat. After five minutes, he heard footsteps approaching. Suzannah eyed him warily from inside.

He held out his hands in supplication. "I swear, I won't take long."

"You have sixty seconds," she said with a quiver in her voice.

Shit. Had he made her cry? Nothing made any sense, but if he only had sixty seconds, he had to act fast. "Please, don't quit. Prairie needs you. If you quit, it'll be months before we find another suitable candidate, and we need a doctor yesterday." She didn't move to shut the door, so he pressed on. "I'll stay away. It'll be like we never met."

His chest wrenched at her grimace, but this was for the best. He'd drive to Manhattan for medical care if it kept her here for the community. After a long moment, she nodded brusquely. "I'll stay," she said in a low voice.

Gunnar let out the breath he'd been holding in a whoosh, but he didn't feel relief. Only emptiness. And deep sorrow for a life that could have been. "Thank you." He turned to go, but stopped at the steps, turning back around. "Your daughter," he said in a strangled voice he didn't recognize as his. "She's adorable." And more than anything, he wished she was his.

He spun on his boot heel and hurried down the walk before he made a fool of himself.

Chapter Four

*S*uzannah closed the door and leaned against it, heart pounding. She pressed a hand against the solid wood in a feeble attempt to still the shaking that now enveloped her.

It'll be like we never met.

She let out a half-hysterical laugh. If only. But then her eyes drifted to the little ball of energy tearing through the living room, making her stuffed cat fly. Her heart, her joy. She'd go through the heartache and pain all over again for Lulah. "Five more minutes, bug," she called softly, not entirely trusting her voice. "Then teeth and jammies."

Lulah stopped and turned, peering at her through her Batman mask. "And stories?"

She was too adorable. All it took was hearing Lulah's tiny voice and the day's troubles melted away. "After teeth and jammies." She left Lulah flying, and returned to the kitchen where Iris sat fretting at the table.

"What was *that* all about?" Iris vibrated with indignation. "The nerve of him coming over here."

Suzannah leaned against the kitchen counter, too

wound up to sit. "Calm down. I think he's as shocked as I am."

"That doesn't excuse what he did."

"No. No, it doesn't. But he's right, Prairie's desperate for a doctor. And let's be honest, I need this to work out, too."

Iris sighed, tucking her dark hair behind an ear. "True, that. But you can always move back in with me. I'm going to be lonely without the two of you."

Suzannah made a face, shaking her head. "You've been too good to us, and I've cramped your style for almost four years. Staying with you was supposed to be temporary."

She'd have been lost without Iris and their other best friend, Bailey, when Lulah'd been born. Those early days had been so difficult… and terrifying. Their solid presence had kept her sane and focused on being the best parent she could be while advocating for a very sick little baby.

Iris waved an arm. "I don't have a social life anyway, so what's the big deal?"

"Maybe it's time you got one. You're a total catch, especially now that we're out of the way."

Iris scowled. "Don't talk about yourself that way. And thanks to you, I've been able to hold off on my parents setting up a profile for me on saadhi.com. Don't laugh," she scolded as Suzannah bit down on her lower lip, shaking. Iris's parents had been hounding her for years to find a husband. "You know it's true. My parents already think I'm too old."

"Well, I don't. You're only a year older than me."

"Exactly – but that's like a hundred in Indian years. And they're having trouble accepting that I might be permanently happy single."

"Are you?"

Iris nodded. "Yeah. I've got my kiddos, and I love the

organizing I'm doing for the teacher's union. And I want to come down here and visit you as much as possible."

"Lulah'd love that. She's going to miss you."

Iris gave her a look that Suzannah knew only too well. The *I don't care that you don't want to talk about it, but we're gonna talk about it anyway* look. "What do you think you're going to do?"

Suzannah's gut churned. "Did you hear what he said on the porch? That he'd stay away. That it would be like we'd never met."

"You have to tell him."

"He doesn't deserve to know," she shot back with a bitter edge.

"That may be the case, but he *will* find out. It's a small town. People will ask questions. And if he has any math skills at all…" Iris gave Suzannah a meaningful look. "It's gonna be waaaaay worse if you hold out."

"But what about Lulah? How's it going to affect her to suddenly have a dad in her life? And furthermore, it will devastate her if he's a flake. How do I know he won't run out on her like he did me?" Pain shot through her heart. If she didn't know better, she'd suspect valve trouble. But, no. This was heartache, pure and simple.

Iris's eyes filled with compassion. "You can't keep her wrapped in cotton and wool forever. She's a tough kid. And she has us."

"But she's been through so much already. More than any child deserves." Her throat tightened, and she was dangerously close to bursting into tears.

"I know," Iris soothed. "But you'd be foolish to let him find out through the gossip mill. You're gonna have to trust that she inherited a large measure of her mama's strength. She'll be fine, no matter what."

Suzannah blinked away the tears as Lulah flew into the

kitchen, still wearing her Batman glasses and cape. She gathered her baby, her life, into a protective hug. "C'mon, bug. Let's get you into those jammies. You can play Batman again tomorrow."

"And catch bad-guys?" She gazed up with a heart-melting smile that reminded her too much of the devastatingly handsome cowboy who'd just been at her door.

"You bet."

When they'd completed their nighttime ritual of jammies, teeth-brushing, three stories, and hugs and kisses for Iris, Suzannah sat down on the floor next to Lulah's bed. These moments were quite possibly her favorite of the day. Holding Lulah's tiny, pudgy hand, she sang to the tune of Twinkle, Twinkle, Lulah's high voice blending with hers.

Jesus, tender shepherd, hear me
Bless this little lamb tonight
Through the darkness, be thou near me
Keep me safe 'till morning light
Jesus, tender shepherd, hear me
Bless this little lamb tonight

Lulah turned her big blue eyes toward her. "We didn't look for stars, yet."

"Tomorrow."

"Promise."

"One for Mama, one for Daddy, one for Iris, and one for Bailey."

"And yours in the middle, surrounded by everyone who loves you." She kissed her daughter's forehead and cheek.

"Do you think my daddy will know how to find us?"

There went that pain in her heart again. "Because we moved here?" She could barely get the words out.

Lulah nodded, looking very concerned.

"Yes, bug. Your daddy always knows where you are, and he loves you very much." Tonight, the lie ate at her. Before, it had always been easy to imagine Gunnar somewhere out in the ether, and that in a parallel universe, maybe he loved his daughter. It had been easy to assure her baby that both her parents loved her, even if one couldn't be with her. But what now? Fear clawed at her. Would Gunnar break Lulah the way he'd broken her? All her protective mama bear instincts said *no*, she couldn't let him do that to her baby. She'd give her life for Lulah, do anything to keep her safe, whole. *Happy*.

"You haven't listened to my heart, yet."

"Don't worry. I haven't forgotten." She'd never forget this part of their nightly ritual. Suzannah couldn't sleep at night until she'd assured herself that Lulah's heart beat strongly and soundly beneath her ear.

Lulah's hands threaded through her hair, as she dropped her head to Lulah's tiny chest. It always took a second to adjust her hearing when she didn't use a stethoscope, but there it was. The telltale *lubDub, lubDub, lubDub*, pumping blood through the heart chambers and out to the rest of Lulah's tiny body. Just as it should. The constant anxiety Suzannah carried, eased a fraction. But only a fraction. After everything they'd been through, part of her lived in dread that at any moment, the other shoe would drop.

Chapter Five

*S*uzannah pushed back from her desk with a sigh, rubbing at the knot in her neck. To say the first days at the clinic had been hectic, was an understatement. Long hours of setting up records software, providing physicals for literally everyone – students and adults alike. Some of the people she'd visited with hadn't seen a doctor in years. She'd given vaccinations, prescribed high blood pressure medication, removed warts, and suspicious moles, and confirmed a pregnancy for a very scared teenaged girl.

Rolling her shoulders, she exhaled hard and fast, then repeated the movements. Her phone buzzed on the desk.

Iris: *Did you eat lunch?*

She glanced at her unopened lunch sack, guilt rippling through her. If it weren't for Iris, she'd be twenty pounds underweight. She quickly typed back. *Eating now*

Iris sent back a slowly-faced emoji. She deserved it. It was nearly three-thirty. But this was the first break she'd had all day. She wasn't about to keep patients waiting while she stopped to eat lunch. Suzannah dropped into her chair and reached for her lunch. She pulled out an apple just as the bell sounded, alerting her to a visitor. With a heavy sigh, she replaced the apple. Lunch would have to wait a bit longer.

Smoothing her slacks, she pushed through the door to the waiting room. A woman about her age paced the floor, face screwed up in deep thought. "Can I help you?"

The woman started, and whirled to face her. "Uh, hi. Yes. Um… I'm looking for Dr. Winslow?"

"That's me." She smiled, hoping it would put the woman at ease. "Is there something I can help you with?"

The woman glanced around. "Is there somewhere we can talk?"

"Of course. Can I get you to fill out an intake form first? My receptionist is on break." Suzannah walked around to the receptionist's station and rifled through the papers, looking for a clipboard.

The woman waved her off. "Oh, no. I'm not here for a check-up. I-I just wanted to talk." The woman rushed on before Suzannah could direct her to a seat. "I'm Amy Goodwin. I'm a midwife, and I work with many women in the area."

Ah. That explained it. She was all too aware of the politics between physicians and midwives. She'd been witness to some very intense showdowns during her residency. One irate doctor had even called the police when a midwife had transported a patient for care.

Amy continued, a spark of challenge in her eye. "I want to remind you of the Kansas State Supreme Court ruling in the eighties regarding childbirth and midwifery. I'm a lay midwife, and in this state, I'm allowed to deliver babies.

Suzannah couldn't help but smile. She admired the

woman's spunk. "I'm aware of that, but thank you for the reminder."

Amy's gaze narrowed. "What's your position?"

"On home birth?"

Amy nodded, gaze guarded.

"Women have been giving birth for centuries without modern medicine. Birth is a natural event, and in most cases, provided disinfecting protocols are observed, is low-risk and can take place anywhere."

Some of the tension left Amy's shoulders. "Would you be willing to be a back-up for me?"

"I think we should get to know each other, before we agree to that kind of a relationship," she said cautiously. "But I'm not opposed to it. But this facility isn't equipped for c-sections. And we don't have an anesthesiologist."

Amy nodded. "I've thought about that. In the past, I've moved my higher risk patients, and my Nervous Nellies to my guesthouse, closer to Manhattan."

Suzannah nodded, impressed. At the same time, wishing that the facilities here were more extensive than a few patient rooms attached to a gym. Prairie needed a full-blown medical center – complete with x-ray and MRI machines, and a surgery unit. But given what she'd seen of the town since she'd arrived, that day was far-off, if ever. The town, the county, simply couldn't afford it. "How many patients do you have currently?"

"I don't feel comfortable with more than twenty. But there are more than twenty women pregnant around here. I've referred some to a midwife I know in Manhattan."

"I'm happy to take on patients as well," Suzannah offered. After a pause, she asked Amy a question that had been eating at her for days. "So, is it my imagination or are there lots of young, *really young* women who are pregnant?"

Amy made a face. "More than I like. I mean, every

baby is a gift, but yes, there are three girls at the high school who are currently pregnant."

"Has anyone thought of offering a community health class?"

Amy perked up. "Dottie Grace has been bugging me to do one for months, but I just don't have time."

The wheels in Suzannah's brain began spinning. "You know, I gave several community health talks during my residency. It's part of what drove me to consider rural family practice."

"There's so much misinformation out there, and not just about sex."

"I agree," said Suzannah. "I'll talk to Dottie. Maybe I could give a talk one evening."

"The diner would be the perfect venue."

This time, the women exchanged a genuine smile. Something hooked in Suzannah's chest. Maybe she'd just made her first friend in Prairie.

Chapter Six

Staying away from Suzannah lasted all of two weeks. Two agonizing, sleep-deprived weeks, where Suzannah's face had dogged him at every turn, sleeping or waking. Taunted him when he caught a flash of blonde hair at Millie's organic grocery. Ten days in, he'd finally caved, and Google searched her. He'd looked four-and-a-half years ago, trying to piece together what had gone wrong, but at the time, she'd had no social media presence. It was like she didn't exist. Of course, he'd been searching for Suzannah Harper, not Suzannah Winslow, daughter of the multi-gazillionaire and media personality, Orrin Winslow. Everyone knew the wild success story of Orrin Winslow. His grandfather had made millions running hooch during prohibition, and then invested in oil. Orrin, in turn, had invested in real estate and a few tech companies that had exploded in value. The Winslow name was on buildings from Chicago to Dallas. As soon as he typed in her name, an engagement announcement from the spring after Vegas popped up. "She didn't waste any time," he'd muttered, acid rising up his throat. But he had to look. The announcement was only a paragraph – detailing that a fall wedding was planned, and that the bride-to-be was just about to begin her medical residency. The lucky asshole? Dalton Cavenaugh, CEO of a local biotech company about to go public.

He'd kept to the horses, after that, working himself to exhaustion every night so that he could collapse into dreamless sleep. But even that didn't keep his mind from dwelling on the little girl in the Batman mask and home-made cape, with the white-blonde hair like her mother's. And then to the pain in his chest at the thought of what he could have had. Which made no sense, because he didn't want it. Rephrase that. He hadn't wanted it with anyone except Suzannah.

Yeah. Fucking mess.

Days later, he led his new mare, Sugar, out of the barn to where Parker sat atop Ricky, one of Gunnar's favorite horses. "You have the post-digger?" he grunted.

Parker motioned to the equipment covered in canvas and strapped to the back of the saddle. "Yep. And wire cutters."

"The spool's out where we need to make repairs." Gunnar mounted up and urged Sugar out of the barnyard, taking a northeasterly track away from the creek that separated the Hansen property from the Sinclaires.

"I also have a bottle of chill-the-fuck-out," Parker called from behind, laughter lacing his voice.

"I'm fine," he snapped.

"And I wear curlers to bed at night."

Even Parker's attempt at sarcasm wasn't enough to force a laugh. "Let's just get the work done."

Parker pulled abreast and shot him a speculative glance. "Dude. I think you need to get laid in the worst way."

Sure he did. But the best he could hope for was to rub one off in an attempt to chase sleep late at night. "Not happening."

"Is that because the object of your desire is off-limits?"

"There is no object of desire."

Parker chuckled. "Denial ain't just a river, man. Everyone knows why you've holed up on the ranch like a hermit."

Gunnar's gaze jerked up. "What did you tell Dottie?" he demanded.

"Calm down, calm down. I didn't tell Dottie anything. It doesn't take a rocket scientist to figure out things ended badly between the two of you. So why not man up and go talk to her? I didn't take you for a coward, Gunn."

"For starters, I said I'd stay away. For seconds, there's nothing *to* say. She dumped me and moved on. Had a kid with some asshat named Dalton Cavenaugh."

"So *that's* what's eating at you, isn't it? It's the fact she's got a kid."

Parker always had a knack for saying what others were thinking. And this time, Parker had come dangerously close to the truth. But broken hearts had a way of teaching one how to deflect, and Gunnar was now a master. "You know as well as I do that the hopeful grannies in town, *including* Dottie, would love nothing more than to see me settled down and adding to the gene pool."

Parker gave him a look of understanding. "I swear, every time Cassie complains about being a little tired, Dottie's eyes turn hopeful."

What was it with these older women? "Do you even want kids?" he asked as they reined the horses to a stop a few yards away from the barbed wire spool. In front of them, stretching over the hill, were three rotted fence posts that had fallen during the last thunderstorm.

Parker shrugged as he dismounted. "I don't know, man. Cassie's seen a whole lotta ugly. And I think she's worried about having to give up piloting. To be honest, I'm happy not sharing her. Our time is precious enough as it is, between Guard duty and fighting fires." Parker hesitated. "I've been talking to the Forest Service about certifying our hand crew as a hotshot team."

"No foolin'?" Gunnar looped Sugar's reins over a low hanging oak branch.

"For starters, it would mean a pay raise for all of us."

"But it's also more dangerous," Gunnar filled in as he headed to inspect the rotten posts. "And you'd hate to leave Cassie alone to raise a child."

Parker nodded. "Especially after my near miss."

Parker'd narrowly escaped with his life the summer before thanks to an explosive wildfire. It had taken months to fully recover from his injuries. "I get that. But you know, lately…" He hesitated to say more. But Parker just looked at him expectantly and waited for him to continue. "I'm worried about dad. He's slowed down since his heart attack this spring. It's taken so much more of my time to run the stables. I was thinking of stepping down from the board. Maybe taking a back seat." That would at least spare him from further interaction with Suzannah.

Guilt flashed across Parker's face.

"I'm not trying to guilt-trip you or anything," Gunnar rushed. "You've been invaluable, but if you're moving onto bigger things… maybe I need to hire a foreman, and a hand or two to help with the ranch."

Parker shot him a sardonic grin. "Might free you up to pursue a certain doctor."

"Oh hell, no. Fool me once, shame on me."

"Fool you twice," Parker supplied.

"Right? Never again."

"People seem pretty taken with her," Parker offered.

Gunnar took the wire cutters and snapped the barbed wire, disengaging it from the fence, and taking care to loop it carefully then set it aside. They'd need to run new wire from the spool once the new posts were planted. "But I'm not," he said firmly. "And don't go getting any ideas." Not that he'd ever admit that to anyone, even Parker. But deep down? Part of him wondered if this wasn't his great second chance, and that he was blowing it by staying away. Especially during Sunday dinners, when he heard his parents and Hope gush about how lovely she was, how smart, how compassionate. That was more like the Suzannah he'd fallen for, and not the woman who'd crushed him at the altar. "Let's get this job done."

The afternoon sun beat down on them, sweat burning their eyes and soaking their shirts. They worked quietly, efficiently, slipping into a familiar rhythm born of years of working side by side. Parker had always been like another brother to him, even more so now, with Axel living in Oklahoma. And if Parker didn't think hiring some help was a bad idea, maybe it was time to approach his father. Hansen Stables had been run solely by the Hansen family for generations. On the one hand, it didn't seem right to bring in outside help. On the other, the work of keeping the property in the black was simply becoming too much. By hiring a foreman and some local hands, Gunnar could focus his energy on further diversification. Take a page from the Sinclaire playbook and look into eco-tourism, or hospitality. They'd managed both successfully, as well as the paintball course both families worked together. "So I've been thinking…" Gunnar started, pulling tight on the wire and wrapping it around the new post.

"About the doctor?"

Gunnar ignored the jibe. "City folk are pretty curious

about a working ranch. Why not upgrade several of the bunkhouses, and offer excursions? Visitors could help with ranch work."

Parker grunted, wrestling with the new fence post. "Could work – *Look OUT!*"

Before either of them could react, a weak spot in the barbed wire snapped and the strand came whipping toward Gunnar's face. Without thinking, he used his arms to shield his face, and the razor-sharp barbs dug into his skin with a fiery bite. Pain streaked up his arms, stealing his breath. "Fuck," he muttered as the warm metal scent of blood hit his nostrils.

Parker was next to him in an instant, whipping off his shirt and pressing it to his arm. One look at his face told Gunnar all he needed to know. "It ain't pretty, is it?"

Parker's face pinched with concern as he shook his head. "We've gotta get you into town asap. Here." Parker took his other hand and pressed it to the shirt that was rapidly turning red. "You need to press as hard as you can."

A tendril of fear snaked through Gunnar. "Did you get a look?"

Parker shook his head. "No. I wanna stop the bleeding first. Raise your arm over your head. I think we should walk back. And press as hard as you can."

Gunnar nodded as the first wave of searing pain hit him. Better he was with Parker than anyone else. By the time they reached the barnyard and Parker's truck, Gunnar's arm burned from holding it over his head. "Not exactly how I'd imagined seeing Suzannah again," he remarked wryly.

"Be damned glad she's in town." Parker kept his eyes on the road, pushing his speed.

"Don't let Weston catch you going that fast."

Parker didn't answer. Shit. Gunnar glanced up at his arm. The shirt was soaked with his blood. He exhaled slowly, shutting his eyes as a wave of nausea churned his belly. He didn't do blood. "Stay put," Parker ordered when he skidded to a stop in the parking lot of the clinic. In a flash, he was out of the truck and around the front to open the side door. "Keep squeezing that arm."

Gunnar swung a leg out of the truck, and stumbled as he landed.

"I've got you," Parker said, grabbing his shoulder.

Parker ushered him through the doors. "Where's the receptionist? I thought you guys hired a receptionist?"

"We ran out of funds." he gritted out.

Parker slammed his hand on the bell at the counter. "Hello?" he shouted. "Doc?" He banged on the bell repeatedly.

Seconds later, Suzannah flew out, face a picture of calm. Until they locked eyes. Once again, she blanched.

Through the haze of pain, Gunnar gave her a weak smile. "So we meet again."

"Second door on the left," she barked, a small tremor in her voice. "What happened?"

"Barbed wire," Parker supplied. "We were repairing fence posts. Profuse bleeding, possible radial artery cut."

"Did you take a look?"

Parker shook his head. "I was about ten feet away when the wire came flying. Blood started pouring pretty fast. I thought it best to apply direct pressure and get him in as fast as possible."

"How long ago was this?"

"Maybe half-hour? We were on horseback, and there was no way to get him mounted without taking off the pressure. And he couldn't have ridden."

Suzannah made a face, but nodded. "Okay, let's take a

look then. Let me wash up. Parker, you too? I may need some help. There are surgical gloves in the box next to the sink."

Seeing her in action jolted Gunnar from his haze of pain. Her hair was pulled back into a simple ponytail, and even the scrubs couldn't hide her luscious curves. "Let's see what we've got here. Gunnar?"

Her touch sent an electric shock through him, causing him to suck in a breath.

"You okay?" Concern flicked across her face. "What's your pain on a scale of one to ten?"

For a broken heart? Definitely a ten. "Five," he managed.

"Hmm. Your face says otherwise. Can we remove the cloth?" Her voice was like a goddamned Siren. Soothing, hypnotic. He was lost to her spell, and no amount of lashing himself to a mast would save him.

He winced as the cloth lifted.

"Parker, there's a container of chlorhexidine in the upper cabinet, along with some chux." She peered at him, eyes soft. Gunnar's chest squeezed into a painful knot as a memory of her sated and soft in his bed shimmered before him. So much nicer than the cold, angry, suspicious expression from a few weeks ago. "I need you to lay your arm on the exam table. We need to clean it out."

He nodded, not trusting himself to speak. Instead, he focused on the pain radiating up his arm, letting its sharpness fill his mind, blocking out all other thoughts.

"Parker, can you brace his wrist?" She glanced at him again, eyes filled with concern. "This is going to hurt. Try and stay as still as possible?"

He nodded. Whatever was coming, it couldn't possibly hurt as much as his shattered heart in the aftermath of Las Vegas. He grunted as the liquid hit his arm. Okay, maybe this hurt close to that. He shut his eyes and braced for more. Cleaning the wound probably took less than thirty seconds, but the agony seemed to go on forever. Bringing him right back to the day he kissed her goodbye. He glared at her.

"I know," she answered sympathetically. "It's almost over." Suzannah took a gauze cloth and dabbed at his arm, inspecting the four-inch-long jagged, open wound. She made a noise in the back of her throat, and probed the wound.

"*Ouch,*" he snapped.

"I know, it hurts. I'm sorry. I just need to make sure you didn't nick the artery." After an excruciating moment, where Gunnar listed every curse word he knew, forward and back, she placed clean gauze over the wound, then took his free hand and placed it firmly on the pad. "You'll need stitches, but it looks like it could have been much worse."

He smiled grimly, holding her gaze. An emotion he couldn't name flickered in her eyes, a little spark of something that set his heart pounding and his arm throbbing.

The alarm on Parker's phone started sounding. "Shit," he said after checking it. "Someone's spotted a brush fire west of town. I've got to get to the fire station. Will you be okay getting home?"

Gunnar nodded. "Just do me a favor and let my folks know I'm okay. Tell dad it's just a scratch."

Suzannah snorted. "You're not going to be able to do any heavy lifting for a couple weeks – you don't want to risk popping the stitches."

Now it was his turn to snort. "Two weeks?" He shook his head. "No way. I've got a ranch to run."

Her gaze snapped to his. "Is he always this stubborn, Parker?"

Parker snickered. "Depends. The Hansens have been known to engage in acts of hard-headed idiocy from time to time."

Again, her mouth quirked, and this time he recognized what was in her eyes. Heat. Just a flash, but it was there. Pure, unadulterated heat. His pulse kicked up a notch as awareness shot through him.

"I'm outta here, Doc," Parker said as he pulled open the door. "Let me know if he gets out of hand."

Suzannah gave him a wry smile. "I'm sure I can take him if he does."

Parker shut the door, his laughter echoing as he walked down the short hallway to the exit. The air between them charged, silence looming between them. Gunnar's good hand twitched with the urge to reach for her. "Suzannah." He didn't recognize his voice. It came out strangled, pained.

Her face contorted. "Don't do this, Gunnar."

"Do what?" he pressed. "Acknowledge there's still something between us?" Pain had a way of stripping away all pretense. "Tell me you don't feel it, too. I dare you."

Chapter Seven

*S*uzannah retreated to the far corner, opening and closing cabinets and drawers with an intensity that belied her calm. "Let's focus on getting your arm sutured."

So that's how she was going to play it? Gunnar fought a wave of disappointment. Hell, it was his own damn fault. He was the one who'd promised to stay away, act like there was nothing between them.

"I'm going to have to give you a couple of shots of lidocaine. You'll want to be numb when I sew you back together."

"Just stitch me up. It can't hurt more than it already does," he grumbled.

Her eyes jerked to his, the barest hint of a smile making the corner of her mouth twitch, before looking right away again. "Posturing doesn't impress me." All her attention seemed focused on arranging several instruments on a small tray. "You should know that," she murmured.

"What impresses you, Suzannah Harper?"

Her eyes sparkled like the gaudy chandelier above them. "Straight talk. Kindness." She said it with such a wistful note in her voice, Gunnar knew she'd been hurt. Even though he barely knew the mysterious beauty in front of him, he could tell that her heart was pure, true. And he wanted to punch the lights out of whoever had betrayed her trust.

"Then you won't take offense when I tell you I'd very much like to kiss you?"

Heat flared in her eyes, and she bit down on her lower lip, mouth turning up at the corner on one side. "I'd like that. Very much," she answered, echoing his words.

The world dropped away when his mouth touched hers, desire rolling through him as they tentatively explored each other. Bringing a hand to her neck, he deepened the kiss, flicking her lower lip with his tongue, nearly groaning when she opened, and he tasted her sweetness. This was it. She was it. He knew without a doubt this was the woman he'd marry.

The memory acted like a sucker punch. "Maybe I don't like needles," he muttered, heat racing up his neck. But why reference their first kiss? Unless she couldn't stop thinking about the two of them, either.

She turned back to him giving him a sympathetic look. "You're not alone. Most people don't watch. You can shut your eyes if you like."

Except that he couldn't look away. Not from her, not when every movement she made acted like a tractor beam.

"When was the last time you had a tetanus shot?" she asked after she'd disposed of the needle.

Gunnar shrugged. "No idea."

"Alrighty, then. I'm going to recommend a tetanus shot while we wait for the lidocaine to do its job."

Suzannah slipped out the door and returned a few moments later with another syringe on a tray. Her movements were swift, perfunctory, as she pushed up the sleeve of his tee and swabbed the top of his arm with alcohol.

"Take a deep breath and slowly blow it out." Her voice caressed him, soothed his rough edges, took him back to a time when she whispered dirty words in his ear. He didn't even feel the sting.

"You're good at that," he said with a little too much gravel in his voice.

"I've had a lot of practice." She moved away again, and he immediately felt the loss of her. "We should be done in a few minutes," she said with a faint wobble in her voice.

Gunnar might have missed it if he hadn't been focused on her like a laser, but it was definitely there, and part of him thrilled at the recognition. She put on a headband with a light, and clear glasses, then wheeled over a stand covered with sterile pads and a tray filled with instruments that looked more like torture devices than medical equipment. His stomach lurched at the sight.

"I'm going to recommend you don't watch," she said firmly. "You're numb, but it's human nature to flinch." She narrowed her gaze. "Do I need to bring you a bucket before I start?"

"Hell, no," he growled.

Her mouth quirked. "There's no shame in keeping one close by."

"I'm ain't gonna puke." His stomach gurgled, contradicting him.

This time, she giggled, a sweet sound that made his insides go funny. "You sure?"

"Just do it. I'll shut my eyes."

"Alrighty, then." She flipped on the light, put on clean gloves, and bent her head.

Gunnar shut his eyes and clenched his abs. No fucking way was he going to humiliate himself by puking. No matter how awful his stomach felt.

"You'll do better if you breathe in and out slowly through your mouth," she commented. A moment later she spoke again. "Inside stitches are done."

He hadn't felt a thing. "You're fast." The whole thing surprised him.

She chuckled again. "Like I said, I've had lots of practice."

Four and a half years. Four and a half years of her life he knew nothing about. Except that she'd had a baby and at one time, had been engaged. "Who was Dalton Cavenaugh?" The question popped out before he could stop it.

She froze.

He risked opening an eye, then promptly regretted it. She looked guilty. A nasty green fog crept through him. Had Dalton been her boyfriend all along? Had he been nothing more than a wild fling before she settled down? He ground his teeth at the thought.

"I... now's not the time," she answered with a bite in her voice.

Gunnar tensed. "When is the time?"

"*Sit. Still,*" she snapped, without lifting her head.

The air crackled between them. Gunnar's thoughts tore through him like buckshot. He couldn't believe she'd faked everything between them in Vegas. Lying didn't suit her. She'd never come across as a manipulator. Even now, he could read her emotions as clear as day. But what if he'd just been a fool? Had been looking for something that was never there? But kisses didn't lie. He'd kissed enough women to be sure of that. And she'd kissed him like she'd been in love with him.

"Done." Whatever she'd been holding clattered to the tray. Her hands returned to his forearm, wrapping it in gauze. "You'll need to keep this dry for forty-eight hours.

Then you can shower." She was all business, wheeling her cart to the counter, refusing to look at him.

"The inside stitches will dissolve in two or three weeks. I'll need to see you back here in ten days to look at removing the outer stitches. No heavy lifting *at least* until then. No work whatsoever the first forty-eight hours, and if you insist on working after that, be sure to clean the wound site twice a day." She reached for a pad on the counter and started scribbling. "I'm going to give you a prescription for codeine–"

"Don't need it."

She continued as if he hadn't spoken. "And one for a strong antibacterial ointment. There are all sorts of microbes on a ranch that could give you a nasty infection at the wound site." She held out the papers, then looked up, baby blues filled with turmoil. "Any questions?" she asked with a little catch in her voice.

Millions. Like, *why the catch in your voice?* And *why was I not good enough?* He was almost afraid to hear the answer to the latter. He opened his mouth, then snapped it shut again before he made a fool of himself. He needed to stick to his promise of staying the hell away from Suzannah.

"Do you need a ride someplace?"

So tempting to say yes. He shook his head. "I'm good, thanks."

"Here." She rifled in the drawer and walked over to where he stood, holding out a card. "Don't hesitate to call if you have any questions, or if the wound changes color. It will be red and swollen the first couple of days. If it gets hot, or you get a fever, I want to know about it right away."

He took the card, fingers brushing against hers. Electricity shot up his arm. Her tiny gasp registered somewhere in the recesses of his brain. She'd felt it too. "I bet he never kissed you like this." Before he could stop himself, before

his right mind shouted *what the fuck are you doing, asshole?*
Before rational thought slammed on the brakes, he'd taken
her mouth, claiming her with a possessive ferocity that
brooked no arguing.

In the eternity that stretched between one second and
the next, she stiffened, and then melted into him with a
groan, kissing him back with equal anger, equal fervor,
tongue battling his as she clutched his shirt.

This was too much, too intense, and yet they both
threw fuel on the fire consuming them. Keeping his mouth
on hers, he walked her back to the door, bracing his
injured arm above her head, slipping his other hand
underneath her scrubs to find the soft flesh at her middle.
She yanked his shirt from his jeans, scraping her fingernails
along his lower back, before sliding her hands beneath his
boxer briefs to cup his ass.

She angled her hips to press her pussy against his erection, and he swore he could feel her heat melting the brass
of his zipper. "Suzannah," he groaned, running his fingers
along the sweet curve of her spine.

"No talking," she bossed, reaching for his belt.

So... she wanted a hate fuck? An angry, hot, winner
take all, pounding until they were both exhausted fuck?
He'd give her everything she wanted, and more.

He nipped at the sensitive spot he remembered existed
a little below and just behind her ear. Her skin tasted
sweet-salty, and he caught a whiff of her perfume, a
heady combination of jasmine and citrus. Something
hooked deep in his chest at the recognition, like a part of
him he'd locked away had stepped back into the light. He
caressed the curve of her breast, reveling in the fullness,
thumb sweeping across her already aroused nipples.
Rolling one between his thumb and forefinger, he took
her mouth again, inhaling the moan that came from deep

in her throat. Her hips rocked against him, seeking friction.

She worked his zipper down and reached into his shorts, taking the length of him. Gunnar's eyes nearly rolled back into his head, it felt so good. Like a homecoming. "Hell, 'Zannah," he said, slipping and calling her by his pet name for her. The one she'd admitted no one ever called her.

"I said no talking," she growled low and sweet, capturing his lower lip between her teeth and biting gently while she gave a gentle upward tug on his cock. Electricity raced up the back of his legs, settling in a fiery ache deep in his groin. He had to regain control of the situation fast, or she'd bring him to his knees in seconds.

Gunnar offered a silent prayer of thanks for scrubs. One pull on the drawstring, a quick yank, and he was staring at pale pink lace. He inhaled sharply – he'd been the one to introduce her to sexy underwear, and the discovery she hadn't reverted back to cotton boy shorts sent a ripple of satisfaction through him. He'd never look at her scrubs the same way again.

She whimpered, sliding her thumb across the slick head of his cock. He got the message. Now was not the time for subtlety. He went straight for the elastic, peeling aside the thin fabric to expose her sweet pussy. Fuck. She was soaked. The scent of her arousal hit his nostrils, and he buried his head against her neck, inhaling deeply and dragging his tongue down to her collarbone. "Tell me you missed this, 'Zannah," he ground out, sliding a finger into her slick heat. "That no one makes you come the way I do," he said, throwing her words from years ago back at her. He was overcome with a primal urge to claim her, to mark her as his, to remind her how good it had been between them.

She answered with a cry, and a roll of her hips, but no words.

Not good enough. Not this time. Not after the hell he'd been through. "Say it." He rubbed her clit, sliding her arousal over the protruding nub. Her hips bucked and she moaned, bearing down on his finger. He slipped in another, scissoring and stretching her, filling her the way she used to beg to be filled. "Say it," he said roughly.

"Yessss," she hissed, glaring at him, eyes snapping.

He grinned at her, before taking her mouth again, plundering her sweet recesses and letting her ride his fingers. But they weren't done. Not by a long shot. And he wasn't about to let this be a one-way pleasure street. Sweeping his tongue against hers one last time, he broke the kiss, breath coming in short, harsh gasps, and he slipped his arousal coated fingers from her. She cried out with a scowl.

"Look at me 'Zannah."

She lifted her eyes, hazy and glittering with lust. Gunnar's breath snagged. She was damned hot like this, cheeks flushed pink, hair pulling from her ponytail, mouth swollen and soft. All the reasons why he hadn't been able to stay away from her the first time around came flooding back. He touched her lips, like satin under the pad of his finger, and coated them with her essence. She gasped, eyes widening slightly, then bit down – hard, cleaning her arousal from his finger like a kitten with a bowl of cream.

His cock jerked under her grip, balls aching with the need to bury himself deep inside her. "Tell me you've got condoms close by, beautiful." Desire roughed up his voice. He couldn't help it. She twisted his insides into a knot.

Suzannah jerked her chin toward the cabinet. "Upper left." Her voice came out strangled, desperate.

Gunnar kissed her again, deeply. Tasting a hint of her

sweet, salty musk. "Don't move." He stepped back, cock bobbing out of his jeans like a flagpole as she released him. He found a fishbowl of condoms on the top shelf, and tore one open, sheathing himself with his good hand. Returning to her he braced his good arm above her head. "Take off your shirt. I wanna see those glorious tits."

Keeping her gaze locked with his, she whipped off her top, then paused, hand hovering over the front clasp of her lacy bra.

"You're gonna have to take it off if you want my mouth on you," he cajoled. Her breasts had always been sensitive, and on more than one occasion he'd brought her to orgasm only by teasing her nipples.

A determined look flashed briefly across her face, and she flicked the clasp. Gunnar's heart nearly stopped. Her breasts were as luscious and full as he remembered, but he'd been utterly unprepared for the effect that they had on him like this. The creamy flesh was streaked with tiny silvery stretch marks, and her nipples stood prominently in the center of rosy dark pink circles. Jealousy tore through him. He'd wanted this, wanted her to be the mother of his children. To see her body swollen and ripe with his seed, to see her nursing their child. Someone, not him, had been the lucky one. And that someone, that *asshole*, was no longer in the picture. Who left a woman like Suzannah high and dry?

The angry, jealous monster in his head told him it served her right. But that wasn't who he was. Not really. He'd been raised to be a caretaker. A provider. A goddamned gentleman. And good men didn't leave women to struggle alone. By God, even if it killed him, he'd help her. However he could. And if she let him, he'd give her as many orgasms as she requested. Maybe that made him a pushover. For certain, it made him a damned fool. But he couldn't stay away from her.

He lowered his head, tracing a silvery stretch mark with the tip of his tongue, down to her aureole, across her nipple standing tall, begging to be cherished. He licked and sucked, flicking it until she writhed against the wall. "Gunnar... *please.*"

"Please what?"

She answered by wiggling and shimmying until her pants dropped and she kicked a leg loose and hooked it around his hip, centering her pussy over his cock. Another memory came crashing through to the present. A dark hallway, a slinky pale dress hiked over her hips, a red patent leather stiletto digging into his ass. He'd always appreciated her height, how perfectly paired their bodies were, as much then as now. And quite frankly, she was sexier in scrubs and tennis shoes.

He teased his cock at her entrance. God, he'd missed this. Missed *her.* Missed the way she fucked with glorious abandon, completely giving over to her baser desires. Missed the chemistry that exploded between them like an ancient oak brought down by lightning. He'd never admit it, but she'd ruined him for anyone else, and he wanted to savor this reunion – as fucked up as it might be. How many nights had he awakened, dreaming of her taste on his lips? Her cries of ecstasy echoing in his brain? "Please what, baby?" He slid his cock through her slick folds, rubbing her clit. "Tell me what you want."

Another growl, laced with impatience. "You. Inside me. *Now.*"

Her words sounded like music to him, and never had he been happier to oblige. Using his injured arm, he traced a path along her hairline, down her jaw. Tipping her chin, he swiped a thumb across her lip, marveling at her, momentarily struck by the wonder of seeing her again. An ache closed his throat, but just as quickly, he swallowed it back and steeled himself. This was a fuck with an old flame. Nothing more. The bond they'd once shared might be broken beyond repair, but he could at least make this good for both of them.

Keeping his gaze locked on her, he slowly pushed into her tight heat, giving a silent fist pump at her gasp then sigh. "That's right. You remember how good it feels, don't you?" Her eyes lit, giving her a wild, unfettered and other-worldly aura.

"Watch your arm," she ordered, voice high and soft.

"My arm is fine," he gritted, thrusting his hips and smiling at her moan. Truly, he felt no pain. It might hurt like the devil later, but he was being careful, only using that hand to caress her and take her higher. He gently pinched her nipple, balls drawing tight as she bore down on his cock and pulled her leg tighter against his hip. She met him as a partner in this wild dance, hips rolling to meet his thrusts, heat building between them like an out of control prairie fire until they were both slick with sweat.

With a long keening wail, she seized around his cock, face frozen in the most beautiful expression of ecstasy. It was too much for him, and he followed her over the edge with a guttural cry, emptying himself into her until his vision hazed. He touched his forehead to hers, not quite ready for the moment to end. Her arm wrapped around his neck, and she offered her mouth for a kiss. He complied, then stepped back, reluctantly, to dispose of the condom.

When he turned back around, she gave him a sated smile, the angry snap in her eyes finally gone. *Thanks to a thorough fucking.* His chest puffed at the thought.

"I don't think I can feel my toes."

He chuckled. "Like, I said. I bet Cavenaugh never kissed you like that."

Her eyes fluttered down, and pink tinged her cheeks. "We never kissed."

Gunnar cocked his head. "I don't follow."

She rolled her eyes. "Dalton and I never kissed. He's an old family friend and not my type."

Not her type? Gunnar fought back the spark of hope that flamed in his chest.

She continued, face growing pinker. "My mother planted that announcement. My parents… have certain expectations. And she thought by publishing something in the Star, she could manipulate me."

Gunnar's mind whirled. She'd never been engaged to Cavenaugh? Never kissed him? So there must have been someone else? Not Cavenaugh and not him, then who? Heat raced up his spine as the sick feeling returned to his belly. He wasn't leaving the clinic until this got sorted once and for all. And then, if the asshole who left her to fend for herself was still living, he'd hunt the motherfucker down and introduce him to justice Prairie-style. "Then what lowlife knocked you up and left you high and dry?"

She met his eyes with a half-defiant, half-scared look. "You. You're Lulah's father."

Chapter Eight

*I*f someone had told Gunnar that the Pope was a trannie from Ohio who believed he was the Virgin Mary, and that Jesus lived on Mars, he'd have been less stunned than he was at that very moment. Shocked didn't even *begin* to cover what was happening in his body. His hands grew cold, his lips went numb, and the ringing in his ears became so loud he couldn't think. "Excuse me?" His insides felt like they'd been turned outside his body and hung out to dry. He stumbled back into the exam table. "Are you fucking kidding me?"

He was a father??!?

Part of him wanted to punch something. He'd always been the one who'd imagined having children, passing on the family legacy to his sons and daughters, because of course, he was going to have a big family. Yet he'd been the one sidelined, fated forever to be Uncle Gunnar. Never *Daddy*.

And now Suzannah was standing here telling him he was a father? The sense of loss nearly cleaved him in two. He'd missed out on all the milestones he'd imagined sharing with her when they discussed babies in Vegas. A host of pictures flew through his mind – Suzannah, belly swollen with *his* child. Laboring and delivering *his* child. Without him. Nursing and caring for *his* child. Rolling over, crawling, first words, first steps, *everything.* A weight pressed down on his chest, making it hard to breathe. His mother, God, his mother. She'd been so excited when his niece Melody June had been born. So hopeful, so filled with joy. The knowledge that she'd missed out on every first with a first grandchild would kill her. How could Suzannah do that to him? Keep him in the dark this way? Deny him what they'd talked about, dreamed about when they'd been together? So many moments, gone forever.

A bigger part of him wanted to laugh, to spin her around in his arms and carry her, carry *them* home. He'd build a princess palace for his little girl, show them he was the knight in shining armor they'd been missing this whole time. He'd push his little girl on his childhood swing that still hung from the enormous oak tree in the front yard. He'd teach her to ride, and give her a pony. Or ten. The dream he'd held closest to his heart, had finally come true. "You mean we've been everything we've both wanted *this whole time*? That we're a family?" He shouldn't feel this excited, but that adorable little girl with the Batman mask and the white blonde waves was *his.* "I want to meet Lulah. It's short for Talulah, right?" Gunnar started through a mental checklist. "My bunkhouse is too small for us, but it would only take a few months for me to put on addition. In the meantime, I could commute. Stay with you, and help with Lulah."

Suzannah's face froze, a picture of surprise and shock. Then her forehead creased. "I– I'm not sure that's a good idea right now."

"What do you mean, it's not a good idea? We're a family, and I want to meet my daughter."

"Of course you do, but I think we need to discuss some things before–"

A tendril of fear snaked through his belly. "Don't keep me from her, Suzannah. Not after all this time. Not after I bared my soul–"

"Gunnar. Stop." She spoke sharply, holding out her hands. "Slow. Down."

His heart pounded in his ears. "What? What's wrong?"

She let out a surprised laugh, shaking her head, then grew serious. "Before I let you see Lulah, we need to talk."

"What do you mean, *let me*?" That got his hackles up. "She has a right to know her father."

Suzannah straightened. "She absolutely does. And the fact of the matter is that it's been four-and-a-half years, Gunnar. And my number one job is to keep Lulah safe. And I don't know you."

"What do you mean?" His voice rose. "You know me better than anyone."

"Do I? Do I really?"

"What's that supposed to mean? Do you think I'm some kind of a creeper?" The thought of anyone hurting his daughter churned his gut. If anyone laid a finger on her… God help them.

She lifted a shoulder. "I wouldn't be a good parent if I didn't vet you."

That offended the shit out of him. "You've got to be kidding, right? I'm her goddamn father, 'Zannah."

"And let's be honest, Gunn." Her voice steeled. "We knew each other a total of four days. *Four Days.* How well can you know a person in four days? You could be an abuser, for all I know."

Or an axe murderer. Axel's voice of reason sounded in his

head. Still, the thought she lumped him in with scum of the earth, stung. "But I'm not."

Her face softened. "So we need to not jump into things like before."

It was too much, all of it − the joy, the hurt. He couldn't think in here. The room felt too hot, too small. He needed fresh air and space. He needed someplace to wrap his head around the atomic bomb that had just detonated above him. "I've got to go. I'm sorry."

He pushed off the exam table and brushed past her, fumbling with the door and bursting into the hall. In the back of his head, he registered her voice calling after him. But he just… couldn't. Not right now. He stumbled out into the late afternoon sun, and started walking. He'd walk all the way home if necessary.

His feet ached, and the sun was setting by the time he reached his bunkhouse. His arm throbbed, but he didn't care. He went straight to his laptop and googled *toddler car seats*. Holy shit. Pages and pages of ads and articles came up. He gulped, clicking on a safety report first. He grimaced at the picture that loaded, of a car seat on the side of a road next to a mangled car. Icy fingers grabbed at his heart. What if something happened to his baby girl? He drove an old truck. Was it even safe? For the next three hours, Gunnar slid down a rabbit hole of heart-stopping fear. Is this what it meant to be a parent? That you went through the world scared shitless and looking for danger at every turn? He glanced around his modest bunkhouse. The outlets were exposed. The carpet was old, and probably not fire-resistant. Hell, was any carpet fire-resistant? Maybe he should switch it out for hardwood. Or tile. Definitely tile. Not flammable. But what if she fell and hit her head? His stomach churned sickeningly at the thought of

Lulah, sprawled on the floor, in a pool of blood, Batman mask askew.

He jumped up from the chair. He had to get out of here. Get some fresh air and get a goddamned grip. In three steps he was out the door and heading through the trees to the other side of the barnyard, out to the hills. Without thinking about his direction, his feet naturally carried him north, along a path he'd traversed since he'd been not much older than Lulah. Guided by nothing but the moon and memory, he trudged toward his destination, a lone oak that stood just below the tallest hill on their property. For as long as he could remember, it had been a gathering place of sorts. They'd buried his Uncle Warren's ashes on the east side of the tree, so that for eternity he'd be greeted by the first rays of sun.

His heart sank as he approached and realized he wasn't alone. But who was it? The figure stepped out from behind the tree. Of course, his cousin Maddie. "Hey, Mads," he called softly, so as not to startle her. "You okay?"

She hiccupped. That answered his question. She'd obviously been crying. He hurried the last steps to the tree, rounding it to give her a one-armed embrace. "I know. I miss the old bastard too."

She laugh-cried, burrowing into him. "Sometimes it hurts so much. And tonight, Henry gave me this look that was pure Dad."

"Blake know you're here?" Blake was her husband, and knowing him, he'd be worried to death if she'd just disappeared.

She nodded. "He suggested I walk up here."

"You married a good man, Maddie Jane." He and Axel had had their doubts about Blake at first, thanks to a decades-old disagreement between the two families, but he'd never seen Maddie happier. Or his sister, Hope, who'd married Blake's younger brother, Ben. "Do you mind if I ask you a question?"

Maddie rubbed her eyes, nodding. "Of course. Do you want to sit? I'm not quite ready to leave yet."

Gunnar threw himself down on the ground, just outside of the edge of the tree. He always preferred being able to see the stars.

"What happened to your arm?"

"A little disagreement with some barbed wire. Took a few stitches."

"From the doctor?" The implication in her voice was hard to miss.

"Nope. Did it myself with whiskey and dental floss," he deadpanned.

Maddie socked him in the shoulder, laughing. "You are so full of shit." A pause. "Hope said you had a fling with her a few years back and you still have the hots for her."

"That so?" He loved how the rumor mill worked. "How'd she hear that?"

"It depends on who you talk to. Dottie and Gloria McPherson said you had a knock-down-drag-out at the diner, but they could see the sparks flying. Parker told Cassie who told Hope that you'd been all over each other when you took your dude's trip to the NFR's a few years back."

Relief melted into his bones. At least Parker hadn't disclosed the worst of it. "Yeah... you could say that."

Maddie turned, eyes narrowed. "Wait a minute." Oh shit. Maddie's mind was like a steel trap. Scratch that. She was a freaking super-genius. Nothing got past her. "Isn't her daughter almost four?"

Thank fuck it was dark, because he was sure his face was on fire. He nodded, grunting noncommittally. "I was hoping to talk about Warren."

"Not so fast, buster. That little girl is a Hansen, isn't she?"

Boom.

And if it had taken Maddie less than six seconds to put two and two together, it wouldn't take the rest of the town much longer. All the emotion he'd been holding back came pouring out of him. "I had no idea until a few hours ago, Mads. And I don't know what to do. Suzannah wants 'to talk'," he made air quotes, "before she lets me meet her."

Maddie didn't react, she just nodded. "And?"

"And I'm mad as hell that I didn't know about this before, that she didn't find me and tell me, because I've never wanted anything more than what y'all have – a family. And I wanna make this right, and I want to be her daddy." His voice caught.

Maddie made a sympathetic noise. "There's more to this, isn't there?"

Maybe it was his shock from the day, or that the pain in his arm was fuzzing his judgment. Or maybe it was just that he was tired of holding it all in, and Maddie had always been like a sister to him. But in the shadow of the moonlit tree, the whole sordid story spilled out, hard and fast like an April downpour. He couldn't stop it, and he didn't want to. When he reached the end, he heaved a rugged sigh, spent.

Maddie's hand came to his back. "You know what Daddy would have said?" She put on her best Warren imitation. "Son, you just gotta march over there and tell her what's what. You be the man she's been missin' this whole time."

Her imitation brought a lump to his throat. "And then he'd tell me to go eat a slice of pie."

She nodded, pinching the bridge of her nose. "Exactly." She half-sobbed, laying her head on his shoulder. "God, I miss him."

"I know. Me too, stubborn ole cuss."

They sat in silence for a long time, the soft night air enfolding them like a blanket. The wonder of it all stole over him. He'd made a baby with Suzannah, and he would do whatever it took to prove himself worthy of the title father. The universe had handed him the opportunity of a lifetime with the woman he'd loved more than any other, and he would not blow this chance at making a family. Fear be damned. The past be damned. Suzannah and Lulah were his to worry about now, his responsibility to provide for. First and foremost, he was a Hansen, and the Hansen men had always stepped up, always cared for their own. Resolve strengthening, he cleared his throat. "Will you help me buy a car seat? I wanna do this right, and I don't even know where to start."

Maddie's arms came around him in a fierce hug. "I need to drive into Manhattan tomorrow, why don't you come with me?"

Chapter Nine

ext evening, Gunnar slowed his truck to a stop in front of Suzannah's little bungalow, and checked the dashboard clock one last time. The green lights read five-thirty. Surely, she'd be home from the clinic by now?

He glanced over to the passenger seat. Three large colorful gift bags sat overflowing with clothes, dress-up costumes, books, blocks, and puzzles. He'd naturally gravitated to anything pink, but Maddie had very quickly set him straight, so many of the items were gender-neutral. Except for the pink princess dress with the sparkles and the matching tiara and wand. And the green and pink fairy wings. *And* the enormous pink pillow unicorn. A daddy had to give a few frilly things to his little girl. Even if she ended up playing with lassos and batman glasses. Nothing wrong with girls wanting to be Batman, no sirree. If his baby girl wanted to be a crime-fighting superhero in a black cape, he'd help her every step of the way. In fact, he'd found a second pair of Batman glasses, and a belt to go with her homemade cape.

He hopped out of the truck, jammed on his straw Stetson, and rounded the front, opening the passenger door. The unicorn went under his injured arm. Next, he looped the bags in the crook of his elbow, and last, he bent to retrieve one of Dottie's chocolate cream pies.

Pie fixes everything. Dottie's words echoed in Gunnar's head as he marched up the walk. How many times had he heard that mantra over the years? Pie fixes everything. Would it be enough to fix things with Suzannah? Would it smooth the way to starting over, this time on the right foot? He rolled his shoulders back, and sniffed in a quick breath, zooming in on the doorbell. His heart pounded with the same half-thrilled, half-sick anticipation that he'd had the first time he'd stepped into the round pen with a wild mustang. He had the feeling Suzannah's bullshit meter was as sensitive as a horse's. One wrong move, and you could lose a horse's trust forever. By his estimation, he'd already made a couple of wrong moves with Suzannah. He needed to prove to her once and for all he could be her man. She and Lulah could count on him, no matter what.

He pushed the bell once, heart pounding way up in his neck. The old-fashioned chimes reverberated across the porch. The seconds dragged on for hours. The door swung open, and Gunnar forgot to breathe. Suzannah exchanged her scrubs for yoga pants and a soft, very clingy, very touchable pink tank top. She'd taken her hair out of her signature ponytail and piled it on top of her head in a messy bun, tendrils hanging down at odd intervals. She looked like a piece of candy, waiting to be licked, devoured. Her eyes widened in surprise, and her hand flew to her mouth. Her eyes crinkled at the corners like she was amused. "What is this?" she asked, voice muffled by her hand.

Was she laughing?

He held out the pie. "I didn't go overboard, did I?" he deadpanned.

She shook her head, eyes sparkling. "You're crazy."

He flashed her a grin. "Does that mean you'll accept my peace offering?"

She shook her head again, eyes darting from the pie, to the gifts, to his face, and back to the pie. Maybe the pie was working. Still shaking her head, she took the pie. "I don't know what to say."

"How about, Come in Gunnar? Have some pie."

A soft giggle escaped, and he gave an internal fist pump. He'd take giggles over scowls any day. She rolled her bottom lip under her teeth, and his cock jumped to life. Even in her uncertainty, sensuality poured from her. And a thousand dirty pictures jumped into his head detailing all the creative ways they could taste the chocolate cream pie she held in her hand. Could she read his mind? The arc of electricity that jumped between them and the heat that flared in her eyes for no more than an instant, made him think so. He shifted his weight under her intense stare, arm starting to throb.

"Okay."

She nodded, and Gunnar melted in relief. Step one, accomplished.

"Lulah's over at the park with her friend Dylan and his mom. We have about thirty minutes."

Not nearly long enough, but he'd take it.

She stood in front of the screen door, holding it open, and he swore he heard her whisper something under her breath. It sounded a helluva lot like *so hot*. He fought a grin as he turned around and stepped out of her way, following her through the living area to the kitchen. The house was laid out like most of the bungalows in Prairie, main living area, small kitchen and dining to the left, with a door to the back yard. In front of him, a short hall leading to a bathroom and two bedrooms. Perfect for a little family.

She placed the pie on the table and gestured to a chair. "Thank you. For this," there was a little tremor in her voice, as if she didn't quite know what to make of all of it. "But it really is too much."

He set the packages and the unicorn pillow over to one side of the table, not ready to sit. "Nonsense. Nothing's too much for my little girl."

"I appreciate the sentiment, but—"

"I promise I won't spoil her, if that's what you're worried about, but I wanted to do something. I mean, it's not every day you learn that there's an adorable little girl running around, carrying your genes."

That made her smile, but only briefly. "I see." She eyed the pie hungrily.

"Dottie said this pie makes people swoon."

The spark of humor returned to her eyes. "Is that so?"

"Yup." He added a nod for emphasis.

"And you're hoping to make me swoon?"

Hell, yeah. Suzannah falling straight into his arms would be very nice. Maybe they could even make a repeat of yesterday. He raked his eyes over her figure, lingering just long enough at the sweet spots to pull a little pink into her cheeks. "Damn straight." He looked her straight in the eye so she wouldn't mistake his meaning. Her cheeks darkened, and a blush began to creep up her neck. This was the Suzannah he remembered, flushed and rosy with arousal, soft and pliant under his hands.

The tension sizzled, building as neither of them spoke. Who would blink first in this battle of wills? Suzannah's mouth dropped open, her breathing becoming more shallow, but in the end, she dropped her gaze, and Gunnar couldn't help but sag a little in disappointment.

"How about a piece of pie?" she asked, still breathless, and she pushed away from the table.

Gunnar didn't answer as she pulled drawers and opened cabinets, grabbing what she needed. He was content to admire the way she moved with such efficiency. She was direct to her core, in words and action. He'd always liked that about her. But why hadn't she been direct with him in Vegas? If she'd gotten cold feet, why not just say so? They'd have worked it out. He gave himself a mental shake as she sat down with forks, paper towels, and plates. He had to let it go. Somehow. He'd moved on from it years ago. Or at least he thought he had, until she'd burst back into his life.

Suzannah cut the pie into eight perfectly equal pieces with the precision of a surgeon. Four neat slices, perfectly intersecting, no wobbling to the knife, just clean, confident strokes. She flicked a glance his direction, and handed him a plate, quickly returning her attention back to the pie as she served herself.

The air remained heavy between them. Full of unspoken words and feelings hidden for too long. Again, the desire to know pressed against him from within, expanding in his chest like a balloon. How could they move forward if they didn't clear the air about the past? Even if all he heard from her was the admission that in the end, he wasn't her type. It would hurt like hell, but at least he'd know where he stood. Then he could focus on being a good father to Lulah, and in time, let the rest go. She cut into her pie, head bent, avoiding his gaze. Her fork made it halfway to her mouth, before her eyes darted his direction. Her lovely blue eyes, once filled with passion, and love, now held hurt, worry. Before he could stop himself, the words tumbled out.

"Why did you leave me waiting?"

At the same time, Suzannah reddened and spoke. "Why didn't you wait for me?"

Her fork clattered to the plate, the sound of metal banging against china echoing in the small space.

"What'd you say?" Had he heard her right?

"I said," she answered deliberately. "Why didn't you wait for me?"

"What are you talking about? *I did*. For hours." Taking care to not bump his stitches, he gingerly crossed his arms, temper rising at the memory. "You never came." Try as he might, he couldn't keep the hurt out of his voice.

Her mouth dropped open. He might have laughed at her expression, but the look she leveled at him was one of white-hot fury. "Because I was at the hospital," she yelled back, eyes flashing.

"Why were you at the hospital?" he yelled, fear and guilt roiling in his gut. "What happened? Were you hurt?" The thought of her hurt, even after all that passed between them, still made him turn ice-cold.

She shut her eyes, shaking her head. "No. A drunk driver careened onto the sidewalk and hit five people. I triaged an older man who needed surgery, and his wife asked if I could stay." She gave him a pained look. "I– I couldn't say no. They were celebrating their fiftieth wedding anniversary."

Gunnar's breath caught. "I checked the hospitals for a Suzannah Harper."

"It wouldn't have mattered. I wasn't the one admitted."

Fuck.

Fuckfuckfuckfuckfuck.

Her voice trembled and she stabbed at her pie, then stirred the piece around her plate. "I called. I texted. I begged you to wait, and you never answered. Not once." A tear streaked down her cheek.

Jesus.

This was all his fault.

He wanted to kick something, punch a hole in the wall, anything. He pushed off the table, pacing through the kitchen. "My phone. My fucking phone."

She stared at him, misery etched in the lines of her face.

Fuck. She didn't believe him. "My brother and I were on our way to the chapel with Parker. We stopped in front of the fountains at the Bellagio to take a selfie, and a rollerblader slammed into me, and my phone ended up on the bottom of the lake."

Suzannah's mouth dropped open, then snapped shut again, eyes narrowing.

She definitely didn't believe him. And why should she? The story sounded ridiculous. He held open his hands. "I swear. Call up Parker and ask him. He still gives me grief about losing my phone."

They stared at each other, silence deepening. On the one hand, Gunnar wanted to laugh, give into the giddy feeling that lurked around the edges of his heart. She hadn't ditched him. On the other hand, the hurt, *the outrage*, squeezed the breath from him with its intensity. She, *and his daughter,* had been three hours away this whole time. His heart dropped to his toes. "Is that why... that's why you never..." he couldn't finish his thought. It hurt too much. It was his damn fault he didn't know about Lulah.

She lifted a shoulder, head still bent. "You didn't want anything to do with me, why would you want anything to do with a baby?"

Her words, and the abject defeat in her voice, pierced him like a poison arrow. "You know that's the furthest thing from the truth." He knelt next to her, tucking a stray lock behind her ear, using the tone of voice he usually reserved for scared horses. "I wanted nothing more than to make a family with you, 'Zannah."

She sniffed. "I was so hurt. I didn't, I didn't…" She buried her face in her hands. "This is all such a mess."

Indeed.

Four-and-a-half years of unnecessary heartache, all that time missed out with Lulah. Still, an ember of hope flared in his chest. He scrubbed a hand over his face, blowing out a long breath and pulling himself back into his chair. "What now? What now, Suzannah?"

She studied him, eyes wary, cheeks stained with tears. The air felt heavy, thick. At last, with a shrug, she shook her head. "I don't know. I-I…" her voice caught, and she shut her eyes, steepling her fingers at the bridge of her nose.

A sick feeling swirled in the pit of his stomach. "Does she know about me?" The thought that Suzannah might have told their daughter she didn't have a father, or worse, punched him in the gut.

She let out a deep sigh. "I… it's complicated."

"No shit, Sherlock."

That, at least, earned him a wry smile. "You have a star. If you look at the Big Dipper, you'll see a star in the center. That's Lulah's star, and she's surrounded by the people who love her most." Her voice began to tremble, and she blinked three times. "Me, you, and my two best friends – her aunties – Iris and Bailey."

Gunnar swallowed down the lump of emotion that clogged his throat. He was less successful at blinking back the prickles in his eyes. When he spoke, his voice came out hoarse, not his own. "What have you told her?"

"That you love her, that you're always watching over her, but that you can't be with us right now."

"So I'm dead," he said flatly.

"No, no." She reached over and grabbed his hand. "Not at all. I'd never lie to her like that." Her voice held a note of reprimand.

"Because not telling her about me isn't a lie?"

Her mouth flattened into a thin line. "Gunnar, she's a baby. Children that age don't have the capacity to think in abstracts. I'd always... I'd always thought–" She sighed heavily, shaking her head. She raised her eyes to meet his, a pained expression on her face. "It's an answer she accepts right now, and leaves room for her to ask questions when she's older. I'd never lie to her about what we shared, that she was conceived in love–"

"But you'd lie to her about my existence."

"You don't understand. You grew up wanted. Loved."

"You never told me about your family," he accused, bile surging up his throat. "You never told me anything."

She had the grace to look guilty, but then a look of grim determination settled over her delicate features. "There was plenty you didn't tell me either."

Touché. "Because it wasn't relevant to *us*," he blustered, not caring that by saying that, he'd have to extend her the same grace.

"Exactly. And now it is." Her eyes blazed. "My family is... difficult. At best. I grew up in a house where I was expected to be perfect. Meek. Demure. I grew up in a house where love was a weapon, withheld to bring you into line. And let me tell you something," she uttered with fierce conviction. "There is nothing, *nothing* worse, than going to bed at night feeling like a parent doesn't love you. That you're wasted space, a disappointment." She glared at him, bristling with defiance. "And I will never let my child–"

"Our child."

"I will never let our child go to bed with a broken heart. *Ever.*" Her tone of voice was all mama bear. "So, yes.

I've kept things from Lulah, because she's young, and it's my job to protect all of her. Including her heart."

"It should have been mine, too."

Her eyes glistened. "Yes. Yes, it should have been. But I wasn't about to let you reject her like you rejected me."

The power of her words slammed into him with the force of a tractor-trailer. He bolted from the chair, gathering her into his arms, ignoring the shot of pain that shot up his injured arm. "Baby, I didn't reject you, you have to know that. This whole situation is so messed up. If I'd known, I'd have been there for you every step of the way."

She melted into him, but all too soon, she placed her hands on his chest and pushed. "The fact remains that you weren't."

"But I can be now, if you let me." He didn't know the first thing about being a father, about parenting, except what Maddie had told him earlier in the day, but if his brother and cousin could figure it out, then so could he.

The pained look returned to her face. "So much has happened. I'm not, I'm not sure how to do this. I mean, what if you decide this parenting business isn't for you? You're already so busy. How are you going to make time for a little girl who won't understand if you can't or won't keep your promises?"

"I always keep my promises," he growled.

She arched a brow, face filled with doubt.

"What happened between us was a miscommunication, not a lie." How could he make her see? Make her trust him again? "Give me your hand." He held out his right hand.

"What are—"

"Just give me your hand. Please?"

She narrowed her eyes as if peering into his soul. Just when he was about to drop his hand, she extended hers, lightly touching his palm. His fingers wrapped around hers, fully encasing her tiny hand. She tensed. Did she feel it too? The electric current arcing between them? He placed her hand on his chest, right over his heart. "Do you feel that?" His heart beat a little faster, thudding under her palm.

Eyes wide, she nodded.

"I promise so long as my heart keeps beating, that I will do right by my daughter. And by you." He let that sink in before giving her hand a squeeze. "Do you believe me, 'Zannah?"

Chapter Ten

*S*uzannah wanted to believe him. Wanted to with all her heart. But for four-and-a-half years, she'd built her life around the belief that he'd stood her up, hadn't loved her like he said he did, and she'd done her best to pick up the broken pieces of her heart and move on. And now he was telling her it was all a big mistake? She couldn't wrap her head around that, just yet. Beneath her palm, his heart thumped steady and strong. And the expression on his face, so earnest. Hopeful, even. "I'm not the same person I was."

He nodded. "I know. I'm not either. But I want to be in your life, and Lulah's too."

"I-I want to believe you." His whole body seemed to relax. "But I'm afraid to," she whispered, heat flooding her chest.

His hand squeezed hers, and he dropped his head, shutting his eyes, brows knit together. "I understand."

The resignation in his voice made her throat ache, but she couldn't lie to him.

He raised his eyes, searching her face, and she met his

gaze, unflinching. "Will you give me a chance to show you I'm serious? That I want to be a father? That you can count on me? We can learn to parent together, can't we?"

If it had been any family she was advising in her capacity as a physician, she'd have urged a splitting couple to co-parent for the sake of their children. She could do no less with Lulah. "Yes, of course," she murmured, pulse kicking up a notch when his hand squeezed hers again. The prospect of letting Gunnar into their lives terrified her. Even after all the hurt and the years, her body still responded to him like the pull of a magnet. And if she couldn't resist the pull, resist him, what would happen to her heart if he left again? She locked the door on those uncomfortable questions. She would have to be stronger than that. If they were going to co-parent, she'd simply *have* to resist him. Period. "But we can't..." she pulled her hands from his to gesture between them. "We can't do this again."

Gunnar cocked his head. She could have sworn she saw hurt flash in his eyes before he arched a brow. "That was all you, darlin'. I was just happy to oblige."

She recoiled, stung. "You think that was some kind of a revenge fuck?" To be honest, she wasn't sure *what* it had been. A release? For sure. Temporary insanity? Definitely. It wasn't as if she'd wanted to fuck him as a punishment. That wasn't her style. Actually, fucking with abandon wasn't her style with anyone except Gunnar. And maybe that was the problem. There hadn't been anyone since Gunnar. Not with her insane residency schedule and Lulah as fragile as she was. In the years since Lulah had been born, she'd been an automaton. Switching gears from doctor to mother and back to doctor again, losing any sense of herself as an individual in the process. And then Gunnar had popped back into her life. Six-plus feet of blonde gorgeousness wrapped up in perfectly sculpted, rock-solid muscles with a magnetism that triggered a chain reaction in her body.

"What I *think* doesn't matter. But if you want to keep things strictly business, that's fine by me."

Yeah, she'd definitely pissed him off. His temporalis twitched as he clenched his jaw. "Fine," she huffed, breathing going a little too shallow. "Fine," she repeated for emphasis because she didn't know what else to say. And she needed to say something to fill the awkward silence that had erupted between them. Because this? Staring down your ex-lover, your ex-*love*, and the father of your child after you'd just had full-on angry monkey sex less than twenty-four hours earlier in your exam room? Not awkward at all.

Gunnar spoke first, clearing his throat. "So what, now?"

The absurdity of it all, hit her with the force of a two-by-four. She huffed out a rueful laugh and picked up. "How about we finish that pie?"

Suzannah's heart tripped in her chest. They were really doing this. How in the hell did she introduce Gunnar to Lulah? Without a doubt, Lulah would like him. Where most children who'd gone through the battery of tests and doctors and surgeries she had, tended to shy away from strangers, the opposite had happened with her. Her baby talked to everyone. But how would Lulah react to the reality of a father when the only one she knew was a star?

"Why don't you stay for dinner?"

Gunnar smashed the remaining crumbs on his plate with the back of his fork. "Are you sure? I mean, of course, I'd love to."

She let out another shaky laugh. "We have to start

somewhere, dinner seems like a good place. I-I think you two need to get to know each other before... before—"

"Before we tell her?"

The look of disappointment on his face pierced her in the heart. She nodded slowly. "Can we go slowly? See how she responds? She's not used to men in her life."

He cocked his head, eyebrows high.

"Don't act so surprised," she snapped. "It's not like I had time, *or* inclination." She hated making that admission, but it was the truth. The doorbell sounded. Gunnar's mouth turned up at the corner, and he looked ready to speak, but she beat him to it. "That's probably Dylan and his mom." Saved by the bell, literally.

Gunnar's brows knit together. "Turner? Mom's Addy?"

She nodded. "How do you..."

"She graduated in my class. Married a real chump, too."

Of course, he'd know that. He'd lived in Prairie his whole life. He probably knew the history of every family in town. The doorbell chimed again. "Wait here. Let me try to prepare Lulah?"

He nodded, looking at once hopeful, and like he'd just swallowed a fish bone.

Suzannah hurried to the door. "Sorry to keep you. I've got company," she said as she pulled open the door.

Addy gave her a knowing smile and cocked her head. "That Gunnar Hansen's truck?"

Lord have mercy, people around here didn't miss a thing. Such a far cry from Kansas City. Heat raced up her neck, and she could tell by Addy's reaction her cheeks were flaming. What could she even say? It was sure to be all over town by the next morning that Gunnar had paid her a visit. "Sure is," she answered breezily with a smile.

Addy gave her an expectant look, waiting for more

information. Too damned bad. Let the town think whatever they wanted. He was just over for dinner and to meet his daughter for the first time. No big deal. Suzannah nearly giggled. Just in time, she swallowed the sound, instead, directing her attention to Lulah. "Did you say thank you?"

"Thank you," she uttered, giving Dylan a squeeze.

"And thank you so much for taking them to the park so I could finish my paperwork."

Addy smirked. "Anytime. I'm glad they've hit it off. See you soon." She ushered Dylan down the stairs, then stopped and turned back, taking the steps by two. She spoke low, so no one else could hear. "I know you're new here. But Gunnar... is a catch. I should have dated him when I had the chance."

Oh dear. "I... there's nothing..." she protested with a wave.

Addy rolled her eyes, shaking her head. "Look. Be good to him, 'kay? He's one of the good guys."

Suzannah pressed her hands to her flaming cheeks, trying to collect her scattered thoughts as Addy disappeared down the street with Dylan. "Lulah? Can you please go wash your hands?" she asked faintly. When Lulah returned, she scooped up her baby into a bearhug. "Have fun at the park?"

Lulah nodded vigorously, all smiles. "We played on the slide, and the swings, and we chased bad-guys."

That voice. Her tiny voice melted her every time. "You did? Well I have a surprise for you."

"Oh, goodie."

"We have a new friend, and he's waiting in the kitchen to meet you." Her heart rate must be nearly two-hundred bpm, and her hands trembled. "Shall we go say hi?"

Lulah wriggled out of her arms, and with a little pang,

Suzannah released her. In the not too distant future, she wouldn't want to be picked up at all. Her stomach jumped into her chest as Lulah bounded ahead of her into the kitchen and stopped short, staring at the big man in front of her, patiently sitting with elbows on his knees, a look of pure joy on his face. In the next breath, his face twisted into a picture of pain. Suzannah's chest squeezed in response, and she found herself second-guessing every decision she'd made since she'd discovered she was pregnant. "Lulah, I— I'd like you to meet our new friend. His name is Gunnar, and he's — he's…" *He's your dad.* She took a deep breath, catching Gunnar's eye.

"Hi Lulah," he interjected, voice thick and gravelly. "What your mom's trying to say is that I help with the clinic." He grinned at Lulah, love shining out of his eyes. Suzannah swallowed hard, determined not to cry. Gunnar continued, voice still husky at the edges. "I hear you like Batman."

Chapter Eleven

*G*unnar could hardly talk through the lump in his throat. She was beautiful, a precious little angel staring up at him, through enormous eyes the color of wild chicory. White blonde hair, fine as silk, waved around her tiny shoulders. Her smile was pure Suzannah, but she was obviously Hansen too. He could see it in the shape of her eyes, and in the angle of her cheekbones. He drank her in, thirsty to memorize every detail.

Did it hurt when your heart grew exponentially? If not, he was having a heart attack. He must be having a heart attack, he couldn't seem to catch his breath, and his hands felt clammy. Dread pooled low in his belly. What if something happened to Lulah? What if she got hurt? Or worse? He could hardly breathe, thinking of it. Maybe he wasn't having a heart attack, maybe this dizzy-heavy sensation was his heart beating out of his body. On the outside – exposed and vulnerable. Whatever it took to keep his baby safe, to provide for her and protect her, he would do it. So long as she kept smiling at him like that.

"Would you like to see my Batman costume?"

He nodded, overcome.

She disappeared with the lightness and speed of a fairy, bouncing into the other room. Did kids ever walk? His nephew, Henry, bounced too, everywhere. When did that stop? God, he hoped never. In a flash, he understood all of his parents' comments about the bittersweet nature of growing older, the misty eyes at holidays and weddings. The way his father looked when he held his granddaughter Melody for the first time, and why his mother sometimes still patted him on the cheek. He fought the ball rising through his chest, expanding like a balloon. This throat tickled and grew hot.

"Gunnar? Are you okay?"

Fuck, no. Not remotely. He nodded, not trusting his voice, not daring to look at Suzannah for fear that tears might leak out his suddenly wet eyes. He scrubbed a hand across his face, taking a deep breath. Was this what it meant to be a parent? To be simultaneously scared shitless that something might happen to this perfect being and so filled with wonder and a kind of giddy joy, that you couldn't tell if you were coming or going?

Axel had mocked him for falling in insta-love with Suzannah. But isn't that what was happening? He was falling in insta-love with his amazing, adorable, use all the adjectives in the dictionary daughter? It didn't seem possible. And yet… how could he not?

Lulah came bounding back in, wearing her homemade Batman cape – nothing more than a rectangle of pink fleece covered in black bats and attached to a long black ribbon, and her Batman glasses. She handed him a long, skinny block. "Here. These are your wings." Before he could ask what to do with them, she'd whirled, lifting an identical block in the air and 'flying' out of the room, shouting "We have to go to the zoo" as she hurled herself into the other room.

He looked to Suzannah for guidance, unsure of what he should be doing next. Staying seated? Following her? Flying with a block? Her eyes were soft as she tilted her head toward the living room. "It's okay. She'll show you what to do."

He stood, turning the block in his hands. This shouldn't feel that scary. He'd played with Henry before, tossing him high while he giggled and screeched. But Henry was Henry. He pushed trucks, and played with his stuffed horse. Gunnar didn't have the first idea of how to use blocks to fly. Lulah's bare feet slapped on the wood floor. "Come on," she urged, holding her block high. "We have to go to the zoo."

Off to the zoo he went, carefully following Lulah's lead. He hit the jackpot when he started to make monkey sounds, and in no time flat, Lulah had him on the floor, pretending to be a lion, and then a monkey, until at last, worn out by an energetic toddler, he held up his throbbing arm. "I gotta sit, sweetheart." He propped himself up against the sofa, cradling his injured arm, feet sprawled in front of him.

Lulah bounced right over and settled herself on his lap, as if they'd known each other for far longer than twenty minutes. She studied the bandage on his arm, then pointed to it. "Did my mommy fix you?"

Precocious little thing, wasn't she? But given her mother, Gunnar wasn't surprised. He gave her an indulgent smile. "I guess you could say that."

Lulah pointed to her chest. "She helped fix me, too."

What the heck was that supposed to mean? Fear gripped him. Had something happened to her? Broken bones? Illness? Oh god, *cancer?* "Did she now?" he said when he found his voice.

Suzannah appeared in the doorway, face pinched with worry. Alarm bells sounded in his head. What was going on? Lulah didn't look sick. She had way too much energy to be sick. She seemed normal in every possible way. Still, alarm bells sounded in his head. "Were you sick?" he asked slowly, drawing out each word.

Lulah shook her head and pulled down the neckline of her shirt, revealing a thin, white scar running down the center of her chest. "See? My mama's friend fixted me."

What the ever-loving fuck? For the second time today, Gunnar went hot, then cold. Judging from the white zipper scar that streaked down Lulah's chest like a Harry Potter lightning bolt, his little girl had undergone heart surgery at some point.

At first, he was overcome with bone-melting terror. A fear so strong, he tasted metal in his mouth. Far, far worse than when his Uncle Warren, and later his dad, had suffered heart attacks. This was the kind of fear that made grown men sink to their knees and blubber like babies. Profound relief followed so quickly, his hands and feet went numb. What in the hell happened? Given that the men in his family struggled with heart issues, was this some genetic something that he'd caused? And why hadn't Suzannah mentioned anything beforehand? His gut roiled, the pie sitting in his belly like lead. It wasn't as if she'd had the chance to tell him, the one cognizant part of his brain reasoned. What mattered was that his little girl was okay. For now.

Suzannah gave him a pointed look, as if to say *We're not talking about this in front of Lulah.*

Like hell.

He turned the full force of his ire toward Suzannah,

glaring. "She had *heart surgery?*" And she hadn't told him? That stung. The thought of his baby girl hooked up to tubes and breathing machines, without him to watch over her, killed him. Just. Killed. Him.

"We'll talk after dinner," Suzannah answered firmly.

Oh, they most definitely would.

Suzannah turned her attention to their daughter. "Lulah. Why don't you show Gunnar how you like to color while I cook dinner."

"I want to play Batman."

"You can play more after dinner."

Her lower lip started to tremble, and she crossed her arms, pouting. "No."

Gunnar fought a smile. So she'd inherited a little of the Hansen stubbornness, huh? "I'd love for you to show me your crayons," he cajoled. "And after, I'd like to show you some things I brought over for a little girl I heard lives here. Do you know where I can find her?"

Lulah's eyes lit. "You have presents?"

He shrugged, widening his eyes. "Maybe?"

She still wasn't convinced. Tilting her head, measuring him, she asked, "Do you like pink?"

"It's my favorite color," Gunnar answered, completely serious.

"Can you draw Batman?"

"And unicorns."

Lulah's eyes widened, and she scrambled off his lap. Hauling himself to his feet, he followed her into the tiny kitchen/dining area, and instantly became aware of Suzannah busy at the stove. "Lulah, can you show Gunnar where we keep the paper?" She turned to him, half-apologetically. "Lulah attends the Montessori preschool, and so I've tried to set up the house like the school, where everything she needs is within reach. It helps foster independence."

Ranch kids typically didn't go to preschool, but the idea made sense to him. He remembered doing chores before he'd been old enough to attend school. Lulah pulled a piece of paper from the tiny shelf behind the table, and placed it on the table, even though the table was bigger than she was. She did the same thing with a basket of crayons, then climbed up into a tall chair that allowed her to be at the same level as everyone else. Clever. He stole a glance at Suzannah, filled with admiration. How had she managed all this on her own?

Gunnar pulled out a second piece of paper, and dropped into the chair next to Lulah, making sure to select a pink crayon from the basket lying between them.

"I'm drawing Batman," she announced, drawing an organic shape with a blue crayon that didn't resemble anything close to Batman.

"What should I draw?"

"Horsey," she answered, completely absorbed in her own drawing.

He wasn't the greatest artist, but he could make something work for his daughter. He had a feeling she wouldn't be a harsh critic. He turned his attention to the paper, sketching out something that mostly looked like a horse. Although it more closely resembled a Clydesdale than one of the more delicately proportioned horses in his stable. He pushed the paper to Lulah. "What about this?"

"Make it rainbow," she yelled excitedly.

"Lulah. Inside voice." This from the kitchen.

She snatched Gunnar's paper and waved it. "Lookey, he drawed a horsey."

Suzannah looked over. "Gunnar drew you a horse?" She raised her eyebrows and shot him a look of gratitude.

As if this was a hardship for him. He'd just drawn his baby girl a pony. If he could have danced a jig on the table, he would have.

"Maybe you can draw him a horse, Lulahbug," Suzannah said as she turned back to the stove.

Lulah began to scribble a rainbow over his horse, using long sweeping gestures. He took the chance to study her closely. From the side, he recognized a distinctly Hansen profile. *But that lower lip!* Even in concentration, it stuck out a bit, wrapping over her upper lip. His insides dissolved. How did parents keep any order at all? All he wanted to do was sit and watch his baby. But shit? His mother would slap him silly for sitting there while Suzannah cooked all alone. Pushing back from the table, he joined her at the stove, placing his hand at the small of her back. "How can I help?" His pulse quickened at her sharp intake of breath.

"It's pretty much done. I'm not much of a cook." Again, she shot him an apologetic look.

"I'm sure it will be delicious." Rule number one from Martha Hansen's farm kitchen: Never ever criticize the cook.

She shook her head, a tiny smile curving her mouth. "We had a chef, growing up, and were banned from the kitchen. And then it was dorm food. After…" she let out a sigh. "After Lulah was born, I lived with Iris. You've met her."

The vision of her two best friends, Iris and Bailey, flanking her at the dive bar where they'd first met in Vegas, swam before him. And more recently, Iris's dark eyes shooting daggers at him as she stood protectively in the doorway. "I remember. And Bailey, too."

"Iris is the best cook I've ever met."

"You haven't met my mother." The response was automatic, and maybe it was the wrong thing to say, but it was true. Martha cooked everything from scratch, and had insisted each of her children know how to make a dozen basic meals before they left for college.

Suzannah chuckled, shaking her head. "So you might not want to tell her that I make a mean frozen pizza."

Gunnar shuddered. "Really?"

She swung around, glaring at him, but with a smile making her mouth twitch. "Don't knock it 'til you've tried it." She turned back to the stove and pulled a small pot from the burner. "You can hang the pictures on the fridge."

Gunnar turned back to the table to discover Lulah playing with the big unicorn pillow. Shit. He'd been so taken with Suzannah, he'd completely forgotten about the presents. "What'd you find there?" he asked, joining her at the pile of gifts.

"Is this for me?" Lulah hugged the pillow to her chest.

"Sure thing. Do you like it?"

She nodded, then eyed the other bags. A little tendril of trepidation wound through him. Maybe he'd gone over-board after all. Well, nothing to do but own it and jump in with both feet. He cleared his throat. "Your mama and I…" he slid a glance her direction. Hell, this was uncharted territory. "We used to be friends. And we haven't seen each other since before you were born." He pulled his finger down her cute little button nose, loving that it triggered a smile. "So when we found each other again, and she told me about you, I got excited, and I wanted to bring you some things."

She narrowed her eyes, staring hard at him, still clutching the unicorn. "Are you Santa?"

He belly laughed. "No, baby girl. Not Santa." He pulled one of the bags closer. "You wanna see?" His chest began to flutter. He couldn't wait to see her reaction when she peeked in the first bag. It was everything he'd hoped for, and more. A loud squeal, a princess dress full of tulle and sparkles pulled out. Crowns grabbed, wands waved, paper torn. He glanced at Suzannah. She wore the same expression his mother had on as many Christmas mornings as he could remember. Half exasperated, half charmed. Lulah tore through the remaining bags, squeals turning into yells, then shouts of exuberance. When the table was a sea of clothing, art supplies, books, and mind stimulating games, Suzannah finally stepped in. "Why don't we put this all on the couch? I can sort it later and put it in her bins. Right now, it's past time for dinner."

In short order, the table was cleared, then set, and Gunnar helped bring food to the table. Suzannah apologized while passing out the paper towels. "I know it's not very grown-up."

He dropped his hand over hers. "It's fine, Suzannah. Dinner will be delicious."

Except it wasn't. The nuggets were dry, and the peas and carrots overdone. Some burned on the bottom. But he ate every bite with a smile, and was sure to take extra apple slices. Lulah stirred her vegetables around her plate, ultimately picking out the carrots and leaving the peas, instead reaching for more apples.

"Peas before apples," Suzannah reprimanded.

Lulah scowled, then stuck out her lower lip. "No."

Suzannah looked pained. "You know the rules, bug. Veggies first." Giving Gunnar a meaningful glance, she started in on her own pile of peas and carrots.

He took the cue and began enthusiastically shoving the tasteless fiber balls into his mouth. "Mmm—mmm. Delicious," he said with a big smile.

Lulah frowned and continued to pick at her peas.

Yep. All Hansen. Gunnar would have laughed if

getting her to eat her vegetables wasn't a serious prospect. To be honest, he couldn't blame her. The peas were awful. "Do you have any barbecue sauce?"

She shook her head. "I'm afraid I'm not so great in the kitchen."

"Mayo?"

"Yes." She started to push back from the table, but Gunnar laid a hand over hers.

"Stay put. I'll get it." He stood and made his way to the fridge, but instead of bringing the jar of mayo to the table, he started pulling open cabinet doors looking for anything to make the peas palatable.

"What are you doing?"

"Poor man's barbecue sauce. Hey Lulah," he called as he pulled bottles and spices from the cabinet. "Guess what? I don't like peas either. And you know what will help?"

Lulah stared at him mutinously.

"Special sauce."

Suzannah craned her neck to see what he was doing, but he turned his back while he worked his magic. A little mayo, a little sriracha, a little lime. Some salt and pepper. It wasn't his best work, but it would make the peas go down. A moment later, he returned with the bowl of pinkish sauce. "What is this?" Lulah asked suspiciously.

He raised his brows and grinned. "Try it. I promise you'll like it." He spooned a bit onto Lulah's plate, and then Suzannah's. "It should make the nuggets taste better, too."

"Hey, don't judge," Suzannah answered defensively.

Gunnar's grin broadened. "No one's judging. I might have a few frozen tamales in my freezer." He'd never disclose they were handmade by Luci Cruz, and some of the best Mexican food he'd ever enjoyed. "Here. Give it a try." He dipped a nugget in the sauce and offered it to her.

She took a bite, mouth going wide. "Ohmygod, what *is* that?" Her eyes crinkled and collided with his. In a flash, the mood had shifted from easy to fraught with tension. Slowly, eyes dark with promise, she licked her fingers, then wiped the crumbs from her lower lip, finishing with a swipe of her tongue.

His mouth turned to ash. Fuck propriety, he wanted to leap across the table and lick every last drop of sauce from her mouth.

"Gunnar?" she repeated, a breathy note to her voice. "What's in the sauce?"

He was dangerously near to telling her. Hell, with a voice and eyes like that, she could make any jailbird sing like a canary. There was no resisting her. Somehow, he managed. "Bachelor's secret."

"You'd have to kill me if you told me?"

Or kiss her senseless.

Chapter Twelve

*H*oly hell. Was flirting in front of one's child okay? It would kill him to ask, but he'd consult with Maddie. It must be okay to some degree if Maddie and Blake were expecting a second child, but still, this was foreign territory. Suzannah hadn't reprimanded him yet, so maybe he wasn't too out of line.

She kept staring at him, expectantly.

Oh.

He'd never answered the question. He winked. "Something like that." Then he pointed to the dollop he'd spooned onto Lulah's plate. "Okay, kiddo. Stir your peas in that and take a bite."

Lulah looked mortified, but didn't protest when Gunnar did it for her. He took a spoonful and waved it in the air. "One special spoonful of magic sauce made just for little girls who like Batman. Open wide." He must have spoken the magic words, because to his surprise and relief, she opened her mouth. Gunnar tipped the sauce-laden peas into her mouth, then repeated the action for himself. "Yum," he said with exaggerated enthusiasm.

Actually, the sauce wasn't too bad. He'd give himself a seven out of ten.

Suzannah covered a laugh, but then her eyebrows drew together. "Can I get you some ibuprofen?"

How did she do that? His arm had been steadily throbbing for at least the last hour. Maybe longer. "I'm fine."

"You want to stay on top of the pain cycle. It's likely going to be uncomfortable tonight."

He waved her off, and airplaned another spoonful of peas into Lulah's mouth. "Don't they say laughter is the best medicine?"

"Not when you've had twenty stitches."

Okay, fair point. But he wasn't in so much pain that he needed a pill. At least not yet. "Why don't I clear the table?"

"Oh, it's okay, I'll get it later."

"No, I insist. Ma would tan my hide if I sat here and let you do all the work."

She cocked her head, not hiding her surprise. "Really?"

"She expected all of us to help around the house. Even dad."

"Well, okay. Do you mind if I give Lulah a bath then?"

"Not at all." He hated she looked so relieved. Being here only for dinner had been completely eye-opening. How did she do it all? And keep the clinic running? He stared at her hard, scanning her face for signs of fatigue. Sure enough, on second glance, they were there. The lines around her eyes were a little deeper, the lids, slightly puffy. If he hadn't trained his eyes for years on studying horseflesh, learning to see the mildest inflammation at the fetlocks and forelocks, the slightest hint of unevenness in a gait, he'd never have noticed. She hid it well. But no doubt, she was exhausted.

The dishes took minutes, sped along by the sweet sounds of mother and daughter singing in the bathtub. When he'd finished, he took a seat back at the table, waiting patiently for Suzannah to finish whatever bedtime ritual she shared with Lulah. To his surprise, they returned to the kitchen, Lulah clutching a book. "She'd like you to read to her," Suzannah said softly.

He could only nod, and patted his lap. Yet again, his throat squeezed tight, and he couldn't talk. He wrapped an arm around her tiny body, breathing in the scent of soap and squeaky clean baby. "What do you have here?"

Lulah began to read, every now and then stumbling over a longer word. A goodnight story involving butterflies and fireflies. With every page turn, he took a mental picture, trying but failing to imprint each moment in his memory. He'd remember this moment on his deathbed, even if he missed a few details.

"What do you say?" Suzannah prodded when the book was over.

Lulah twisted, giving him a light hug. "Thank you for my presents."

He was utterly unprepared for the feeling of her little arms wrapped around him. Nothing compared. Not the moment when a wild mustang accepted a harness, or the moment he first remembered his father looking at him with pride. Not even the moment that still vividly lived in his memory – when Suzannah had told him she loved him completely, without reservation. It was like a star had suddenly gone supernova inside his chest. "You're most welcome, sweetpea." He dropped a kiss on the top of her head and caught Suzannah staring at him, a funny expression on her face.

"Time for bed, sweetie pie," she said, extending her hand to Lulah. Turning in the doorway, she cocked her head toward the front room. "I'll be out in about ten minutes. We can talk on the porch."

Before he had a chance to respond, she'd ushered a bouncing Lulah through the doorway. Across the room, he could hear her high voice asking something to Suzannah, and Suzannah murmuring some kind of a reply. Gunnar dropped his head into his hands, reeling. This was too much. How many bombshells could he take in a twenty-four hour period? Not only had he had the most intense sex since, well, ever, he was still reeling from the discovery he was a father. And now this little girl who'd captured his heart in the blink of an eye had a heart condition? He pushed back from the table, needing to move, to do something besides sit. He spied a coffee pot on the counter. Coffee. Coffee would help. A shot from Jamey's crisis bottle would be better, but he suspected Suzannah didn't have a liquor cabinet. Hell, her fridge was practically empty. What were they paying her? Surely enough that she could keep food on the table. She was a doctor for chrissakes. Weren't doctors super wealthy?

He found the coffee grounds and set about making a pot. While he waited, he studied the fridge, and the pictures he'd hung. If he cocked his head sideways, he could see the shape of Batman in her drawing. To anyone else, it might look like a misshapen blob, but he knew better. He especially liked she'd colored the cape pink and green. The pot gurgled a final time, signaling the coffee was ready. Gunnar snagged the drawing from the fridge and gently folded it, placing it in his front pocket. By the time Suzannah entered the kitchen, he had a steaming mug waiting for her. He held it out. "I saw the half-n-half in the fridge."

"Thank you," she murmured, fingers brushing against his as she took the mug.

Why did she look so surprised? It was just a cup of coffee. Again, the lines of exhaustion on her face jumped out at him. "Do you need to sit? You look tired."

She gave him a wry smile. "You get used to it in Med school."

And she'd been parenting solo on top of it. Hadn't her family helped?

She lifted the cup. "This tastes delicious. You'll have to show me how you do it."

"Let me guess, you burn the coffee?"

"Worse. I can diagnose strep by smell, but they never taught us to brew a proper pot of coffee."

"Should we go sit on the swing?"

"I'd like that."

The tension seemed to melt from her shoulders when he laid a hand at the small of her back as he followed her through the living room to the front door.

"How's your arm?" she asked, holding the screen door for him.

Hurt like a motherfucker. "I'm fine."

She narrowed her eyes. "I can tell you're in pain."

"Not anything I can't handle."

"You farmers. You're all way too macho."

"It's a good thing I'm not a farmer then," he chuckled.

Suzannah rolled her eyes, the corner of her mouth tipping up. Gunnar's chest clutched. Conversation with her had always been so easy. Fun, even. She always made him laugh, and not because she was trying. Just... because. "Explain to me the difference between a farmer and a rancher again?"

"We're neither, but farmers farm."

"And ranchers ranch," she answered with a giggle. "That's super helpful."

"Okay, so farmers raise the grains, the vegetables. Ranchers raise the meat."

"But aren't there chicken farmers?"

"Eggs."

She shook her head, smile still threatening to break loose. "I'll get it one of these days. But if you're not a rancher, what are you?"

"Hansens have raised horses since the eighteen-fifties. I'm sure at one point or another we ran cattle, but we've always been horsemen."

"And women," she added.

Damn, he admired her spunk. "Yes, and my sister would be the first to point that out. She's probably the best of all of us." He took a sip from his mug, trying his best not to wince at the throbbing that made his arm feel like it was on fire. He shifted on the swing, to better face her. "So."

She took a deep breath and slowly exhaled, eyes cast down. "So."

Silence spun out between them, the evening air filling the void with the chirps and trills of crickets and night peepers. Fireflies winked on the grass. By all accounts, this should be a perfectly romantic evening. The air was soft, not oppressively hot, like it would be in a few week's time. A breeze whispered through the tree leaves, like the barest kiss on a satin cheek. Gunnar's body stilled, waiting. If necessary, he'd wait all night. This wasn't his first rodeo where scared mammals were concerned. She might not be a horse, but it didn't take a rocket scientist to tell that she was scared to death. He offered a silent thought of thanks to his sister, Hope. He'd learned so much from watching her gentle mustangs. How to just *be* with an animal. How to give a scared horse, or human, space to settle, to develop the beginning threads of trust. Gunnar took another sip of his coffee and concentrated on keeping the swing moving with his foot. He had questions, days' worth, but they'd never get answered if Suzannah was scared, or felt she couldn't trust him. "If you're not ready to talk, I can go," he offered before he could pull back the words.

She jerked her gaze to him. "No, no. I'm sorry…. It's just…" she sighed heavily.

"Start wherever you like. Or tell me to go."

"I don't want you to go," she answered in a rush. "Please." She shut her eyes, and he could almost see her screwing up her courage. "I found out I was pregnant in mid-January, the day of my first residency interview. I was scared to death. Right away I knew I wouldn't qualify for a surgical residency. To be honest, I'm lucky I got matched at all. Pregnancy is… a liability."

Gunnar's chest flamed. That anyone would think Lulah was a liability, made him want to pound someone into the dust.

"Oh don't go looking like that," she admonished, shaking her head. "Do you know how many locals won't see me because I'm a woman?"

Gunnar sat straight up. "*What?* The whole reason we have the clinic is so that people don't have to drive more than an hour to get good medical attention." What the hell was wrong with some of these people? "We're gonna discuss this at the next board meeting."

"Calm down. Just don't be a part of the problem, okay? And if you hear people being assholes, say something."

"Whatever you want, darlin'."

"And stop calling me darlin'."

"Even if I like you?" He swore he saw her cheeks go pink.

"You're head of the clinic board. Whether you like it or

not, people will pay attention to how you treat me. At least in public," she added.

Fuck. His mind raced back to earlier. "Was I an ass?"

She cocked her head. "Only the first night."

Yeah, not his best moment. Heat raced up his neck. "Can I apologize again?"

"No need."

"Anything you want... Darlin'." He couldn't resist teasing her just a tiny bit, and it earned him a gentle sock at the top of his arm.

"Ha. Ha."

He shifted on the swing so he could see her fully. "I swear, Suzannah. I like teasing and all, but I'd never... in public... I respect you."

Electricity arced between them.

"But I'd like to call you darlin' in private," he murmured, tracing a finger along her jaw. He'd call her that and more, if she let him.

Her mouth dropped open, and the urge to bend his head toward hers, to test the waters, grew within him. But he waited too long and the moment passed. She turned her cheek, serious again. "I started having contractions at thirty-four weeks, and went into full blown labor at thirty-five. Lulah was barely five pounds when she was born."

Gunnar's stomach turned upside down. "Holy shit," he breathed.

"I was pretty scared," she admitted. "But the worst part was when they told me her heart was underdeveloped." She repeated the next information almost in a monotone, as if she'd told it so many times, it was now something to just be endured. "She was born with arterial stenosis, which means that one of the main arteries pushing blood through the heart wasn't fully formed. She wasn't getting enough oxygen, and her heart was unable to pump enough blood."

Gunnar stopped the swing. What had it been like for her? All alone? He was freaking out, and yet this had taken place years ago. "So she had surgery."

Suzannah nodded. "Two. But we're keeping an eye on one of her valves. She may need a valve repair or replacement at some point."

"Oh God, this is all my fault," he blurted, looking away.

Her brows knit together. "What do you mean?"

"My family. We have heart problems. Uncle Warren, before he was taken in the tornado, had a massive heart attack. My dad had one this spring."

Suzannah sat straighter. "Some of that could be diet. What do you know of your grandparents?"

"I'd have to ask my mom."

She took a deep breath, and let it out in a rush. "Okay, that's not going to change the present. But you should make sure you're eating well and getting screened for high blood pressure and cholesterol on a regular basis."

It shouldn't turn him on the way it did, hearing her with her doctor hat on, but a frisson of awareness shot through him. "Let me help. Let me share custody with you."

She recoiled as if she'd been slapped. His heart yo-yoed. Why was she staring at him like that? Like he'd asked her to eat a slug?

"I…" she bit her lip, brows coming together, and shook her head. "I don't think that's a good idea. Not now, at least."

"Why the hell not?" He shot back. It was obvious she needed help. Hell, her cooking skills were abysmal, and her fridge was nearly empty.

"You have no idea what you're asking for."

"I don't care. I don't shirk my responsibilities." She might have struggled all this time on her own, but he was here now.

"She's *sick* Gunnar. Are you ready for that? For the financial burden of childhood heart surgeries? The fear of bankruptcy when the doctor tells you your child needs another surgery? Her first surgery cost twice as much as my med school loans."

Her words punched him in the gut.

"Are you ready to lose your family's land, your family's legacy, when the collectors start calling? Because they *will* call. Or the fights with insurance over what procedures they will or will not cover? Or the copays on medicine? Or when insurance denies you the medicine you need?" Her voice came out clipped, frustrated, angry. As if she was reliving all of it.

Gunnar clamped his jaw so hard his teeth hurt. He had a significant nest-egg, but it wasn't enough to cover half-a-million dollars in medical bills. He'd heard through the grapevine of a family over in Marion whose son developed leukemia. They'd had to declare bankruptcy and auction off everything – land, horses, tractors.

She continued. "Are you ready for the constant worry that your child, your *world* is going to be snuffed out in an instant? They have to stop her heart during surgery. Stop. It." She batted at a tear with the back of her hand.

His heart lurched. He was no stranger to loss, and losing his family's land would be devastating. But he was all in where Lulah was concerned. If something catastrophic happened to her, he'd break. "We'd figure it out," he growled.

"Would we?" she asked, eyes shining with unshed tears. "These are the kind of life events that break marriages. I've seen it happen. Marriages that had half a chance, and were on solid footing, crumbling. We barely know each other."

"We knew each other once," he countered.

She barked out a laugh, shaking her head. "Don't be a fool, Gunnar. We were caught up in the moment. We'd never have survived the stress of a sick baby."

He folded his arms, cradling his injured one. "I don't believe that."

She shut her eyes, pinching the bridge of her nose. "Okay, fine. But you have no idea what it's like, what it's *been* like."

Her words sliced him to the quick. "Then let me in," he growled. "Let me help. Let me show you I'm better than you think."

Chapter Thirteen

*W*hen Suzannah showed up at the clinic the following Monday, Gloria McPherson stood waiting expectantly. Suzannah's heart sank. People were showing up at the clinic earlier and earlier, eating into the time she used to catch up on paperwork, and more importantly, billing. She stifled a yawn and took a long slug of coffee from her travel mug. At least the coffee no longer tasted like dirt. Gunnar had taken to setting up her coffee pot every night before he left. It was a small gesture, but one she greatly appreciated. Especially since she'd been burning the midnight oil on administrative work. Pulling a smile, she lifted her mug. "Good morning, Gloria. Is everything okay?"

Gloria returned the smile. "Oh yes, everything's grand. I'm here to help."

"I'm not sure I follow."

Suzannah unlocked the doors, and held one open for Gloria, following her into the cool, dark interior. Gloria beat her to the light switch, then bustled around the receptionist's station and laid her purse on the counter. "It came to our attention that you might need a little office help."

Gunnar.

Although it could have been any number of townspeople who'd been in the clinic since it opened, and seen that there was no rhyme or reason to the waiting room. She'd finally taken to putting a sign-up sheet on the counter, and taken patients the old-fashioned way.

Gloria turned on the computer.

"I'm not sure—"

"There's a bunch of us in the Posse that got together and set up a volunteer schedule. Mondays are my days." Gloria positively beamed. "You'll have me until four every Monday, Nita Cruz is taking Tuesdays, and Bobbie Appleberry, Wednesdays. I can't remember who took Thursdays and Fridays, you'll have to ask Dottie the next time you're in the diner."

"The Posse?" she said faintly, still trying to process that she was going to have help running the clinic.

Gloria gave her a knowing smile. "We older womenfolk still like to have fun, and we've convinced some of the younger women in town to join us. Mostly it's bunko nights and cocktails. But we read books, too. Some of us have grandchildren."

"And the rest of you want them?" Suzannah supplied.

"Oh my heavens, no," tittered Gloria. "I'm not *that* old. My boys are barely out of high school. I'm enjoying my empty nest." She blushed bright pink.

Suzannah bit her lip to keep from laughing. "Well, this is wonderful. Do you have any computer experience?"

Gloria gave a regretful shake of her head. "I can use basic office programs like Word and Excel, but mostly I email. I'm the organist at the Lutheran church, and I teach piano."

Damn. What she needed more than anything was someone to set up the electronic filing and scheduling system. Someone in her interview had mentioned they'd purchased one, but she didn't have a clue about it. She made a note to ask Gunnar about it the next time he came for dinner. "Well, that's okay. I'm glad you're here." She came to the other side of the counter. "There are intake forms on those clipboards to your left." She pointed to the stack she'd set up the night before. "And I've just been going off a simple sign-up sheet for drop-ins."

"Do you have anyone scheduled yet?"

Heat crawled up Suzannah's neck. She hated coming across as disorganized, but there was enough work at the clinic for four people. At least. It was impossible for one person to keep up with it all. She shook her head. "To quote Star Trek, I'm a doctor, not a software wizard."

"Never fear. The ladies and I will get things running smoothly in no time."

Suzannah's heart warmed. "You have no idea how much this means to me. Do you know anyone who's good at billing? Dealing with the insurance companies has about killed me."

Gloria's face scrunched up as she thought. "Hmm. You know, Elaine Kincaid is a whiz with numbers. She used to do Dottie's books, and now she helps her husband Travis with the books out at Resolution Ranch. She just had a baby, though."

Too bad. Help with the books would be a godsend. "Let me know if you think of anyone. I'd sure appreciate it."

The day passed all too quickly with visits for physicals, strep, plantar warts, and even a broken toe. At four p.m. sharp, Gloria knocked on Suzannah's office door. "Can you manage from here? I've got to get home and get dinner ready for my crew."

Suzannah stood and offered her hand. "Gloria, thank you so much. Having you here today was a huge help."

Gloria pulled her into a hug. "We hug around here. At least the ladies do. I hope that's okay."

She returned the hug, albeit a bit clumsily. Then immediately second-guessed herself. Her mother's voice rang in her head – *We don't hug the help*. But Gloria wasn't the help. Gloria was a neighbor, and a volunteer. And besides, when was the last time she'd been hugged by anyone besides Lulah? When Iris had been in town, but that was going on nearly three weeks. She'd love to be hugged by Gunnar. Heck, she'd love to be all sorts of touched by Gunnar, but *no*. The sexy as sin cowboy was strictly off-limits. Even if he set up her coffee pot every evening, and cleaned up the dishes. And stocked her fridge with groceries and fresh produce from his family's garden, and cooked dinner, and, and… The shoe was going to drop, eventually. Wasn't it? No man in his right mind would want to keep caring for her in that way.

Gloria stepped back, eyes searching her face as if she could see every thought. "You okay, honey?"

Her stock answer popped out. "Yeah. Yeah, I'm fine." But something niggled at Suzannah underneath her breastbone. She got the feeling Gloria asked the question out of concern, and wasn't just making small talk. Gloria seemed genuine. Like she cared about the people who were part of her daily life. With the exception of her two best friends, Iris and Bailey, Suzannah's life had been filled with society types that played by different rules. She'd grown up in a world where people used information and feelings as weapons. Who offered platitudes instead of compassion. The unspoken question poked insistently at her. She bit her lip, mustering her courage. "Can I ask you a question?"

"Do you mind if I sit? You sound like you need to talk."

Suzannah shrugged and offered Gloria a chair, then sank into the chair next to her. "Can I ask you about Gunnar?"

Gloria's eyes lit, then crinkled at the corners as a smile spread across her face. "I've known Gunnar since he was kicking inside Martha's belly."

The visual brought a smile to Suzannah's face. "Really?"

Gloria nodded. "Martha and I lived on the same floor in the dorms at K-State, freshman year. She introduced me to my husband, Patrick. I grew up outside of Kansas City and had come to K-State to major in music and theater. Patrick swept me off my feet, and the rest they say is history. So." She propped her chin on her knuckles. "Ask me anything."

This all felt so junior high. But if Gloria had seen Gunnar grow up, then she could be trusted to tell the truth about Gunnar's personality, couldn't she? But where to start? And how to ask a question without coming across as too nosy, or too interested?"

"So is he... ah... Is he a good guy?" she finally blurted.

"The best," Gloria answered without so much as a pause. "Martha raised her boys right. Of course, they had their wild days when they were younger, but you'll not find a pair of men who will drop what they're doing faster than anything to give you a hand. And their sister, Hope? Lovely."

Relief washed through Suzannah. "So he doesn't..."

"Cat about? Not at all. Now the Benoit twins. They like the ladies. But Gunnar?" Gloria's eyes softened. "He's a catch. And a role model for my boys. If I'd had daughters…" Her eyes grew wistful, before she brushed her hands together. "Well, if wishes were horses." Then she narrowed her eyes. "Something happened between you two a while back, didn't it?"

Suzannah nodded slowly fighting a smile. "You could say that."

Gloria stood, and straightened her skirt. "Well, I hope you kids manage to work it out. If I can help you in any way…" She waggled her eyebrows. "You know I'm more than happy to."

"Thank you." Suzannah stood. "I appreciate that. And thanks again for your help today. I appreciate it more than you know."

Suzannah's heart took off at a gallop when she arrived home with Lulah to find Gunnar waiting on the porch steps twirling his hat in his hands. The almost bashful smile he aimed her direction turned her insides warm and made her knees the tiniest bit wobbly. "Hi," she breathed, stopping in front of him. "Fancy seeing you here." It wasn't really much of a surprise, he'd been patiently waiting on her porch steps every weeknight over the last two weeks, usually with dinner or groceries in hand. The first night he'd showed up after their truce with a full roast chicken dinner. Her mouth had watered too much to send him away, and she was grateful to not have to cook. Cooking ranked at the very bottom of activities she enjoyed. She'd been stunned, when on the second night, he'd not only shown up with groceries, but had insisted on making dinner. A garden salad and pork chops had never tasted so delicious. Gloria's words rang in her head, *Martha raised her boys right. He's a catch.* She was beginning to understand why.

Suzannah supposed at some point they'd have to

discuss introducing Lulah to his family, but the thought still turned her veins to ice. How would they feel about a baby born out of wedlock? And who was now nearly four? With a heart condition? Her own parents had never come to visit Lulah in the hospital. Not once. Never even sent birthday cards. As soon as it had been evident that she had decided to live life on her own terms and not the life they'd meticulously planned for her, she'd been disowned. Literally. Cut off from her trust fund and shunned from family functions. Not that she missed the family functions – they'd been miserable affairs at best. And the modest inheritance she'd received from her grandmother had been gobbled up by a mountain of medical bills. She'd planned to use those funds to pay off medical school loans, but with that money gone, she'd ended up in family practice instead of orthopedic surgery.

"I thought maybe you'd enjoy dinner out." His eyes softened to an unspoken plea when they landed on Lulah. "Gino's has Monday night spaghetti and meatball specials."

Lulah clapped her hands, bouncing. "Pasketti! Mama, I want Pasketti. Please?" Her eyes turned up with the exact pleading expression of Gunnar's.

She burst out laughing. They were two peas in a pod, and there would be no doubt if they went out in public that Lulah belonged to Gunnar. The resemblance was clear as day. "Tell me the truth, you're tired of cooking, and you can't stomach my food."

Gunnar's eyes crinkled. "You know I'm always happy to eat your food," he deadpanned. "I'd never turn up my nose at a home-cooked meal."

"Then let me cook tonight."

"I'd rather take you to Gino's."

"Are you sure?"

Gunnar's gaze turned serious. "Sure as shootin'."

"Won't people talk?" She was half-convinced Addy already knew, or at the very least, suspected. The last few times Lulah and Dylan had played together, Addy looked at her like she *knew*.

"They're already talking, sweetheart."

"But what if someone says something?" She jerked her head at Lulah.

"Not worried."

She crossed her arms. "But why now?"

Gunnar's cheeks pulled tight, a look of determination settling on his face. He looked so much like Lulah about to have a tantrum, she nearly laughed out loud. He spoke quietly, but with conviction. "Maybe I want to take... a friend," he gave her a significant look. A look that said he was interested in far more than friendship. "and her very charming daughter out for a nice dinner."

She couldn't deny the reaction that raced through her body at his look. But she still wasn't buying it. "So, is this a date?"

"I'll let you decide that." He slid his finger down Lulah's nose, sending her into peals of giggles.

"Do that again," she squealed.

He did, with a smile that arrowed straight into Suzannah's soul. Holding him at arm's length seemed to grow harder with each passing day. She let out a heavy sigh. "Fine. Let me go change. Lulah, why don't you show Gunnar your work from today?" She handed Lulah the small stack of papers that Ms. Ivy had given her when she'd arrived to bring Lulah home from preschool. Before she lost her nerve, she brushed past Gunnar who'd made room on the steps for Lulah to join him, and entered the house.

When was the last time she went on anything remotely

like a date? And what did one wear on a date in Prairie? People didn't dress up here. That had become perfectly clear the night of her welcome reception. She'd worn wool slacks, and everyone else had worn denim. She only had one pair of jeans, for yard work. In the back of her closet hung a strappy sundress that Iris insisted she bring. Pale pink with flowers, it flowed to her knees, and was perfect for the warm, humid evening. It was the kind of dress that would shout from the rooftops 'this is a date'. Even with an almost-four-year-old in tow. But if people were already talking… and once they saw Lulah and Gunnar together, the rumor mill would kick into high gear.

Tossing her scrubs in the hamper, she slipped the silky material over her head, a little charge of anticipation winding through her. She spritzed on her favorite perfume and slid a pale gloss over her lips. Last, she pulled out her ponytail and looped her hair into a messy bun. That would have to do. Sliding into a pair of leather sandals, she grabbed her wallet and locked up the house. Everyone had told her she didn't need to bother, but locking up was one habit she'd never give up. Behind her, Gunnar's and Lulah's voices mingled with shared laughter. "Ready," she called out and turned around.

Gunnar stopped speaking mid-sentence to stare, eyes roving slowly over her figure. She swore his eyes left a trail of heat down her body. Only when Lulah tugged on his hand, did he drop his gaze. "Tell your mama how pretty she looks, punkin'." His voice held a hint of gravel.

"Mama you're bootiful," she said with a grin, looking just like her father.

"Thank you, both. Shall we walk or drive?"

"It's only about a fifteen-minute walk. I haven't installed the car seat yet," he tacked on.

The admission that he hadn't yet taken that step, stung.

So for all his talk, he wasn't ready to take on parenting duties. She bit back a sigh. Baby steps. "Not ready yet?" She spoke lightly, but hurt simmered underneath the surface.

He looked at her sharply. "I'm more than ready. Maddie helped me buy one. She's the only one who knows about our situation. And don't worry, she won't say anything until I give her the okay. But I wanted to talk with you before I spoke with the rest of my family. As soon as they see me with a car seat, it's game over. The whole town will know in less than ten minutes."

"Oh." Now she felt like an ass. His logic made perfect sense. "I appreciate you wanting to, er, discuss things first."

"After you've put Lulah to bed?"

"Is that why you wanted to take us out for meatballs?" she teased. "To butter me up?"

He gave her an answering grin before swinging Lulah up onto his shoulders. "Maybe?" He turned serious. "And maybe you deserve a nice dinner out for a change."

Double *oh*.

Double *oh* became a triple *oh*, when they entered Gino's Trattoria and Mario, Gino's son who now ran the place, and was easily in his seventies, looked from Lulah to Gunnar and back again, and then at her, understanding dawning on his face. Yep, the cat was now officially out of the bag. But whatever Mario thought, he was the perfect host, and doted on Lulah as if she was his grandchild. Suzannah pushed her chair back from the table. "I'm so stuffed, I may never eat again."

"I know for a fact, you're going to have the leftovers for breakfast."

"No way. I can hold out at least until lunch."

"I may have to drive over after chores first thing tomorrow, and show you how to make a proper Gino's leftover breakfast."

The offer hit her in the belly, making her insides turn liquid. Heat flared in his eyes, and suddenly the air in the tiny restaurant felt too close, too intimate. So she stood. "Thank you for dinner."

She stayed quiet the walk home, only half paying attention to the running conversation Lulah and Gunnar were having about Batman flying over the zoo and what kinds of zoo animals Batman liked to help fly. She was so distracted, she let Gunnar read Lulah *two* books after teeth were brushed. By the time she and Lulah had completed their nighttime ritual of songs and stars, Suzannah could hardly focus. All she could focus on was the smoldering look Gunnar had given her at Gino's, and how it had gone straight to her core.

The last rays of the sun were lighting everything in gold as she stepped onto the porch, pulse thrumming. Gunnar lounged on the swing, arm slung across the back, muscles pulling his plaid shirt tight, legs bunching under smooth denim. Her mouth began to water. Positively edible. "Have a swing?" He motioned to the space next to him.

Problem was, he took up more than half the swing. If she sat, there was no putting space between them. He'd be *right there*. The thought simultaneously set her body tingling and panic running through her. No hanky-panky. *No. Hanky. Panky.* Kissing him would only lead to more kissing, and more kissing would lead to clothing being discarded and the next thing she knew, she'd be fucking this gorgeous cowboy on her front porch, in front of God and everyone else who happened to wander by. Nope. No, no, no.

The words were on her tongue, but dammit if her feet didn't start moving, and the next thing she knew, she was snuggled up next to him, thigh to thigh, rib to rib, his hand making lazy circles on her exposed shoulder, and her clit throbbing madly, begging for attention. How in Haley's Comet, was she supposed to focus on a serious conversation with *that* next to her? His head dropped closer, and he nuzzled her ear, warm breath sending goosebumps cascading down her neck. "'Zannah," he murmured, voice low and husky.

She always melted when he said her name that way. It was like she turned into some kind of zombie when his voice slid over her body like whiskey caramel sauce. She didn't trust herself to talk. She'd give away every lascivious thought that was coursing through her mind right now. Every unspoken desire. "Mmm-hmm?" was the best she could do.

"We need to talk."

"Mmm-hmm?" He needed to stop nuzzling her neck and sending electric shocks from her nipples to her pussy, or there wouldn't be any talking.

"We *have* to talk." His tongue flicked out to the sensitive spot behind her ear. "Tonight." Then he nipped her earlobe.

"Yessss," she hissed, voice paralyzed.

"But I'm having a hard time concentrating."

"Mmm-hmm." She couldn't manage more.

"You look so beautiful."

Her heart flipped like the twisty coaster at Worlds of Fun.

"And I'm wondering if you'll let me kiss you." His mouth landed at the corner of her jaw, the merest feather of a kiss.

All she needed to do was turn her head. Heat was rolling off him, and her body softened, not interested in resisting at all. The spicy scent of his cologne must have aphrodisiac properties, because right now, her brain cells were exploding left and right, like she was high on painkillers. "Yes," she whispered, registering her answer as if it came from far away, from some other Suzannah in an alternate dimension where her baby wasn't sick, and where life was less of a struggle.

He brushed her mouth gently, managing to light it on fire, while barely touching her. Every synapse in her body waited expectantly, ready to combust the second their lips locked. His gentleness made her chest ache, made her impatient to devour him and forget the uncertainty, the confusion, and worry. But he kept a slow, patient pace, as if he was savoring every millisecond of their connection. When his tongue finally slid inside her mouth, licking along her lower lip, she responded with a groan, clutching his shirt and opening to him. Her heart raced, pounding in her ears, and for the first time ever, if he kept up this slow and steady assault on her defenses, she could come from just a kiss.

But he broke it off, bringing his forehead to hers, breathing shallow. When he spoke, his voice was thick and slightly unsteady. "I want people to know I'm Lulah's father."

Chapter Fourteen

---

*G*unnar's heart slammed erratically in his chest, and not just because his dick was as hard as iron from kissing Suzannah. Kissing her gave him courage, and it had taken every last ounce of his courage to say those words.

She pulled away, lips swollen and glistening, eyes kiss-drunk. "What?"

"I want people to know."

"I'm sure they already know. Did you see the look on Mario's face when we walked into Gino's? It took him about half a second to figure things out."

Yeah, he'd seen the look, heard the whispers by the salad station. And hell, maybe bringing them to dinner was his way of starting this conversation rolling. But regardless of what Mario thought, Gunnar wanted people in town, at least the people he loved most, to hear it from him. And he wanted Suzannah to know that he wasn't embarrassed or ashamed. No, he was proud, and he'd do right by Lulah. Suzannah too, if she'd let him. "But I want people to hear it from me. And I want Lulah to know who I am, too," he

116

added after a heavy pause. The meatballs settled like lead in his stomach.

Suzannah's eyes grew wide, and a look of sheer panic crossed her face. "I-I'm not sure about that."

"You can't keep it from her, especially if the whole town knows."

"I-I don't think she's ready."

"I don't think *you're* ready." Frustration added an edge to his words. He understood her desire to protect Lulah, especially given all she'd endured in her young life, but did that protection have to extend to him? "Hey. I'm on your side, here."

Her eyes narrowed skeptically.

"I am. You're obviously a great mom, and Lulah adores you. And I get that you've been through a lot together."

"Everything."

"Okay, everything together. And I want to help. But you have to let me." He stared at her, hard. Willing his words to sink in. "And, you have to trust me."

She looked like she was about to cry. His insides went all soft and gooey. What was he supposed to do if she started to cry? Shit. Horses were so much easier. "Hey," he said quietly, tipping up her chin. "Do you remember when we were in Vegas and we talked about having kids?" Her nod was more like a twitch, but he'd take it. "And what did I say?"

"You said that while I was doctoring, you'd keep the kids with you in the barn," she answered, barely above a whisper.

"And?"

"And that the best education for kids when they're tiny is being outside. But that still—"

He kissed her, just briefly enough to stop her protests.

"I haven't changed. I still think that, and even if it means I come over here and play outside with Lulah, I'll do that. You can still call the shots, although I'd like you to come meet my family on the Fourth. My brother and his wife and new daughter are driving up from Oklahoma. I could show you around, take you and Lulah out for a ride."

"We've never been on horseback."

"Never?"

She shook her head.

"Woman, you do *not* know what you've been missing." His comment drew a small smile, and he'd take that over tears any day. "My mom's going to be over the moon. You have no idea."

She let out a huff of air through her nose, not quite a laugh. "How do we tell Lulah?"

Gunnar shrugged. "How about, hey there sweet thing, did you know I'm your dad?"

This time she laughed outright. "I don't think so."

"Why not?"

"For starters, learning her dad is flesh and blood is going to come as a shock."

"But she likes me."

"She does," Suzannah agreed, nodding her head. "And I know you're not going to like this, but we need to proceed slowly."

She was right. He didn't like it one bit. "But—"

She stopped his words with a finger to his lips, frowning. "Rule number one of parenting. What you want no longer matters. It's about what's best for Lulah from here on out." She stood, tension radiating from her body. "Thank you for dinner tonight."

Damn. Double damn, triple damn. He was being dismissed.

"We'll come on the Fourth. What time?"

Disappointment flooded Gunnar. "Why don't I come over in the morning, and we can go to the parade. You can follow me out after." His words came out clipped. Flat.

"Gunnar."

He jerked his gaze to her, schooling his features.

The expression she wore was one of exasperated patience. "You have to understand why this can't happen overnight."

He nodded, not trusting himself to speak. "I'd still like to come for dinner this week."

"Of course."

Gunnar stewed the whole drive home, and when he'd parked the truck next to the other Hansen vehicles, he hopped out and dialed his brother.

"'Sup, bro?" Axel answered on the first ring. "How's the doc?"

So many things he could say, but he wasn't about to confide everything in Axel. "So she's got a kid."

"Yeah. Heard that from mom and dad. How's your arm, by the way?"

He made a fist, tensing the muscles, then releasing them. "Hurts, but I'll live. Stitches came out last week."

"I get the feeling this isn't a social call."

Gunnar felt like a balloon was about to explode in his chest. The pressure from keeping this to himself the last few weeks had become unbearable. He wasn't a secret keeper. Not usually, and he hated how it made him feel. Especially when he wanted to shout this news from the mountaintops. "She's mine, Axe. Suzannah's little girl is mine."

Axel let out a low whistle. "You sure?"

Gunnar nodded, pacing around the truck. "Yeah. I am."

"But are you *sure?*"

"Meaning did I ask for a paternity test?" he growled.

"Don't you think you should verify?"

"She's not asking for anything. In fact, she's keeping me at arm's length."

Axel chuckled. "I bet you fucking hate that."

"Of course I hate it. This kid…" Gunnar stopped, throat growing thick. "She's… she's…" He took a big breath, picturing Lulah's smile when he tickled her, or pushed her on the swings. "She's incredible. This giant ball of energy, with big blue eyes and a laugh that makes my insides hurt. And she's smart too, Axe. She can already read." Pride surged through him as he talked with Axel. "And I would do anything to make her happy. It's the craziest thing."

"I know what you mean," Axel interjected. "I fell in love with Melody the second the midwife put her in my arms. The whole thing still blows my mind."

"'Zannah's worried about how to tell Lulah I'm her dad."

"Understandable."

"How can you say that?" Gunnar demanded. "She deserves to know I'm her father."

"Of course she does. But she's practically a baby, right? Talk to Haley if you want a different perspective. She was in foster care until she was twelve."

Gunnar raked a hand through his hair. "But I–"

"You're scared. I can hear it in your voice, man. Take a chill pill. These things take time."

"Since when did you get all wise?"

"Since my wife has educated me on the finer aspects of parenting and raising girls."

Gunnar snorted. "Meaning she's kicked your ass a few times."

Axel chuckled. "Yeah. Maybe. But not saying I didn't

deserve it." After a silence, Axel spoke again. "So what about you and the doc?"

"What about us?"

"Is there an 'us'?"

Gunnar's stomach yo-yoed. There should be. When they kissed, he felt like a goddamned superhero, like he could conquer anything. And yet... every time he pressed, she seemed to step back, or at least falter. What if they couldn't be the family he'd dreamed of? What then? His stomach yo-yoed again. There had to be a way. He had to convince her they were good together. He braced a hand on the side of his truck. "Hell, I don't know. I think there could be."

"But?"

"But she's gun shy. And working her ass off. Which is exactly why she should let me help."

"What have you always told me about poorly broke horses?"

Gunnar blew out a heavy breath. "You know I hate it when you throw my words back in my face?"

"Heheheh. That's what little brothers are for. Just keepin' you honest, man."

"Well, fuck you," Gunnar answered good-naturedly.

"C'mon. Just tell me what you know I'm gonna say. What you *taught* me," he added.

"That if you've got an unbroke or poorly broke horse, you establish trust by being present. And it may take a day or a month, but you can't move ahead with retraining until you've accomplished that first step."

"And when the horse pricks its ears at the sound of your voice, and doesn't show signs of stress when you approach, only then can you reach out and touch it," Axel filled in. "So you've just gotta be patient. If there's something worth pursuing between the two of you, she'll come around."

"Since when did you get so philosophical?"

"Student always surpasses the teacher."

"Ha. Ha."

Axel's voice turned serious. "You gonna be okay?"

"Yeah. Yeah," he answered with a heavy sigh. "Just don't want this to go south a second time."

"I know the feeling."

Truth. Axel and his wife Haley had been college sweethearts, and she'd broken his heart. But a little over a year ago, she'd ended up back in Prairie, studying tornadoes, and the rest, as they say, was history. "Thanks, man. See you on the Fourth?"

"Can't wait."

Gunnar disconnected, then sent a text to his sister.

Gunnar: *Hey, can you pop over for a bit? Gotta talk.*

A few moments later his phone beeped.

Hope: *Sure. Everything OK?*
Gunnar: *Yeah. See you soon.*
Hope: *:)*

Pocketing his phone, he trudged up to the farmhouse where his parents still lived, and skipped the back steps, hopping directly onto the porch. The kitchen lights flooded the porch with warm yellow light. How many family meetings had taken place around the old kitchen table? How much ribbing when Hope and her husband Ben Sinclaire had first gotten together? The Sunday dinners back when Uncle Warren had been alive and his cousin Maddie had just started seeing Blake Sinclaire? More than anything, he wanted Suzannah and Lulah to feel the love that emanated from the kitchen, the love that permeated every meal shared there. More than anything, he wanted his little family, unconventional though they might be, to experience the love that lived in this kitchen. Pulling on the screen door, he stepped inside and kicked off his boots. The smell of a fresh pot of coffee hit his nose. "Ma? Pops?" he called.

"In here," Martha called from the living room. "Come on in."

He helped himself to a mug of coffee and called out as he wound through the kitchen to the living room. "Hey, can we talk?"

Chapter Fifteen

*A*t eight a.m. on the Fourth of July, Gunnar hopped the steps and knocked on Suzannah's front door. Already, the air was warm and muggy, not a cloud in sight. Today would be a scorcher. Lulah opened the door, all smiles, and wearing her Batman pajamas and cape. "Mama, Gunnar's here," she called before launching herself at his thighs to give him a hug.

"Well, hey there sweet thing." He patted her back, heart squeezing at her exuberance. "You ready to see a parade?"

"Mama's making Special Breakfast."

"Special Breakfast, huh? Well maybe I can go give her a hand."

Lulah bounced over to her toy box while Gunnar made his way to the kitchen, where the smell of burned bacon hit his nose.

"Need some help?"

She turned, giving him a sheepish look. "I always seem to burn it."

Gunnar cracked his knuckles. "Step aside. The master

is here." He stepped up to the smoky stove and hit the button for the overhead fan. "Do you have a cast iron pan?"

She shook her head, laughing. "I have no idea. Pans are in the bottom cupboard."

He bent, and in the way back, discovered a beat up old pan. "These are the best. A little hot water and elbow grease, and this will be perfect." He moved to the sink, and proceeded to scrub the heck out of the pan, then dried it with a paper towel. "You have any oil?"

She pointed to the upper cupboard.

After he greased the pan, he held it up triumphantly. "See? Good as new. The only pan you'll ever need."

"Really?" She made a face like she didn't quite believe his claim.

"Well maybe not for spaghetti sauce, but pretty much everything else." He laid the pan on a different burner and turned the heat to low. "The secret to good bacon is low heat."

"But won't it get soggy?"

"Nope. The fat needs time to render out. The best bacon comes with patience and a little TLC."

"Sounds like a metaphor for life."

He lifted a shoulder, quirking a smile and accepting the coffee mug she held out. A zing of attraction flashed up his arm as their fingers brushed. "Maybe so." He stepped closer, into her space. Her eyes dilated as she tilted her head, and her breath came faster. Did she taste as sweet in the morning as she did when they were stealing kisses at night on the porch? Her hand rose to his chest, and he stilled, waiting. *Kiss me.* His body tightened in anticipation, breath stalling in his lungs. If he breathed, the moment would be lost, and he wanted to hang onto this with everything he had. A blast of pure pleasure shot through him when she raised herself on tiptoe and pressed her mouth to his. His free arm shot around her, pulling her flush against his body and he teased his tongue along her lips. When she softened and welcomed him with a slide of her tongue, sparks shot off in his head. Kissing her was like lighting off a whole string of Black Cats. Kissing her was more satisfying than the best homemade meal. He could devour her here and now, but not with an unpredictable little girl in the next room. Reluctantly, he pulled away, grinning down at her pink cheeks and swollen lips. "I like making breakfast with you."

She let out a satisfied breath. "Hmm. It is pretty nice."

"The best." Longing darted through him. Why couldn't they do this every day? "Have you talked with Lulah at all?"

Growing serious, she nodded.

"And?"

"It's hard. I don't quite know what to say."

"Well, what *have* you said?"

"When we found our stars last night, I asked her if she missed Iris and Bailey."

Where was she going with this? Remembering his conversation with Axel, he breathed in through his nose and nodded, giving her space to talk.

"And she nodded. And I reminded her how much they love her, even if they can't come visit all the time. And then we talked about the next time they're coming to visit, and how much she loves them."

"Okay."

She blinked rapidly, voice growing rough. "And then we talked about your star. And I... I asked her if she missed her daddy. I've never asked her that before," she said, voice almost unintelligible through her tears.

Stepping back into her space, he wrapped his arms around her.

"I'm okay, really," she spoke into his shirt, then glanced up.

For a moment, Gunnar thought his heart might pound out of his chest. Her face was the picture of agony. "What did she say?" His heart jumped to his throat, cutting off his air.

Two big tears streaked down her cheeks as she bit her lip and nodded. "She misses you, the idea of you, more than I ever realized." She sniffed loudly. "And so I asked her if her daddy was able to come visit her, would she like that."

Fear iced his veins, but at the same time, he already knew the answer, and he wasn't sure what scared him more, the possibility she wouldn't want to see him, or that she would. Could he live up to whatever four-year-old ideas she'd built up about him in her mind? "And?" he whispered.

Suzannah's shoulders shook, and she nodded into his chest, voice muffled when she finally spoke. "She said... she said that's what she wished for."

Gunnar tightened his embrace, throat tickling, chest growing hot.

Lulah came tearing in and skidded to a stop. "Why are you hugging my mommy?"

"Because she needed a hug," he answered with a little wobble in his voice. "That okay?"

She cocked her head. "I need a hug."

He opened his arm, chest about to crack open wide. Lulah snuggled in between them. "It's a Lulah sandwich," she said with a happy smile.

"It's a Lulah sandwich," he repeated, blinking hard.

Suzannah exhaled roughly and stepped out of his

embrace, quickly wiping her eyes. "Wanna help with pancakes, bug?"

"Does Gunnar know how to make shapes?"

"The best," he called out from back at the stove. "Any shape you want."

"What about a dragon?" she asked suspiciously.

"Easy."

"Unicorn?"

"All the time." He crossed to her and swept her up. "If you promise to be very good, I'll let you sit on the counter and watch."

She looked to Suzannah, who nodded. "Just this once."

Lulah clapped when he sat her down. "I want a dragon."

Gunnar removed the bacon to a plate filled with paper towels, drained the grease and put the pan back on the burner. He held out the bowl to Lulah. "I need you to give it a stir for luck."

She managed to stir without slopping batter on the floor, and Gunnar set to work. His little girl wanted a dragon, and by god, he was gonna make her one. He drizzled a shape into the pan and stepped back for her inspection. "Well?"

She wrinkled her nose. "It needs fire coming out of its mouth."

Alrighty, then. He drizzled some more batter. "Better?"

Lulah beamed at him. "Perfect."

His chest grew warm. He'd never expected the smile of his child to hit him like that, making him a total goner. He'd been utterly unprepared for how much her approval meant to him. "So your mom was telling me about your talk last night."

She stared at him, swinging her legs.

"That you miss your daddy?"

She nodded, legs stilling.

"I bet your daddy misses you, too."

"How do you know?" she asked very quietly.

He plated her dragon pancake and set out to make another one just like it. "Because *you* are a very special little girl." His mind returned to everything he'd read online over the past week about toddler development. And the parenting book he'd ordered on overnight delivery. Keep it simple, let them ask questions. His palms grew sweaty as his thoughts raced about what to say next. This was so much harder than he'd imagined, than he'd practiced.

Ultimately, Suzannah rescued him. "What Gunnar's trying to say, sweetie pea, is that he's your daddy. And he's missed you for a very long time."

He offered her a silent gaze of thanks, and she returned it with a watery smile. He turned back to Lulah, whose blonde brows furrowed as she processed Suzannah's words. After what seemed like an eternity, she looked up, breaking into an enormous smile. "You're my daddy?"

Hearing those words from her high little voice nearly brought him to his knees. It felt like his heart was now on the outside of his body. Very fragile, vulnerable to the slightest barb. "Can I pick you up?" He opened his arms, and she leaned forward, letting him catch her up in a bearhug. "I'm so sorry I couldn't see you until now," he rasped. "But I want you to know how much I love you and missed you." Lulah melted into him, snuggling her head on his shoulder. He caught a whiff of her baby shampoo, as fresh and soft as she was. He risked a glance Suzannah's direction, and the knot in his chest squeezed harder. Her hand covered her mouth, eyes glimmering.

Lulah lifted her head. "Does that mean you're going to marry mommy?"

"No," Suzannah interjected firmly from the doorway.

Why did her statement bring a lump to the bottom of his throat? Marriage was a nonstarter, they were just trying to find their way in the here and now. Neither of them was in a position to talk about the future. And yet... In the back of his mind, the possibility was always there, hovering just out of reach. Gunnar bit back a noise of disappointment, focusing on the tiny person in his arms, returning his hug.

"Dylan's mommy and daddy don't live together," Lulah announced.

"Not all mommies and daddies do," Suzannah agreed, nodding her head.

"But Dylan says they don't like each other. They yell at each other."

"You don't have to worry about that, Lulahbug, Gunnar and I like each other just fine."

"Then why can't he live with us?" her voice wavered, and the lower lip that looked just like Suzannah's pushed out.

Suzannah's gaze snapped to his in a silent plea for help. "Well..., it's—"

"There wouldn't be any room here for my horses," Gunnar interjected as relief engulfed her face. "But I'll come over every day, just like I have been. Does that sound okay?"

Lulah's mouth was a full-blown pout, now. "Will you play Batman with me?"

He nodded seriously. "Of course."

"And read me books?"

"As many as you like."

"And draw me horsies?"

"I'll do you one better," he kissed her head. "How would you like to ride a horse?"

She looked over to Suzannah, who nodded. "First you

have to get dressed, and then we're going to go to the parade."

With a wide grin, she shimmied out of his embrace and ran off toward her bedroom. Gunnar crossed the remaining distance to Suzannah, wanting to hug her, but suddenly feeling unsure. He reached for her hand instead, taking her slender palm in his own. He cleared his throat, but the emotion still clung to his chest. "Thank you. I don–"

"Shhh." She placed her fingers over his mouth. "You don't need to say a thing."

He kissed her fingers, pouring all his gratitude into the gesture. Electricity buzzed down his neck, settling deep in his belly. Did she feel it too? The spark that constantly lurked between them? He squeezed her other hand and stepped closer, until they were toe to toe, and he caught a trace of her jasmine and citrus perfume. He brought his fingers to her jaw, tracing along the bone with the lightest touch. "I installed the carseat," he murmured, just above a whisper. "Weston helped me with it, so I know it's safe. I'd like to drive the two of you out to the ranch after the parade. Would that be okay?"

Her lips parted, and her tongue darted out to slick her lower lip. His cock sprang to attention. He couldn't, he *shouldn't* risk a kiss, but the urge to drive his fingers into her hair and devour her mouth, was primal. She leaned into him, eyes fluttering shut. Oh, hell. How was he supposed to resist *that?* "You feel it, too, don't you?" he whispered, mouth hovering just above hers. A millimeter more, and they'd be lip-locked.

"Better kiss me quick, cowboy," she uttered tightly, breath skating across his cheek.

He covered her mouth. But instead of devouring her, the took his sweet time, stroking into her mouth as if they had all the time in the world and not a handful of seconds before Lulah came bounding back into the kitchen. She tasted sweet, a heady combination of coffee, smoky bacon and maple syrup. And sensuous, like a hot summer afternoon filled with promises of tangled limbs and bare skin. The quiet moan emanating from the recesses of her throat, only added fuel to the fire rising between them. He snaked an arm around her back, pulling her tight, and fuck, if she didn't notch her hips against his raging erection, and give a little roll. But as fast as it started, she stiffened and pushed on his chest.

Not even a second later, Lulah popped into the kitchen wearing a flowered sundress and her Batman glasses. Suzannah must have supersonic hearing. All he could hear was the buzzing of desire pulsing through his veins.

Suzannah shot him a look of pure desire, laced with regret, yet somehow managed to sound calm when she turned to Lulah. "Ready for the parade, sunshine?"

How did she do that? Add mommy radar to her long list of impressive traits. And then it hit him with the force of an anvil dropping on his head. He was still crazy about Suzannah. More so now, than when he'd first fallen for her. The thought should have terrified him, and maybe it would have if he wasn't still flying high from their kiss. Instead, he wanted to bask in the sensation, shout it from the rooftops. He didn't care that she burned coffee, or bacon, and cooked horrible dinners. That shit didn't matter. What mattered was he was the luckiest sonofagun in the world. And if it took the rest of his life to show Suzannah and Lulah that he was their man, their champion, he'd do it.

Chapter Sixteen

*S*uzannah fidgeted in the passenger seat of Gunnar's truck as they turned underneath the wrought iron sign reading Hansen Stables. Ever since the kiss they shared a few hours before in her kitchen, Gunnar had been acting strangely. Well, not exactly strangely, but different. Resolute. Grounded. Unflappable. *Confident*, like something major had changed between them.

Of course, things had naturally changed now that Lulah knew he was her daddy. But this felt... deeper. And honestly, she was so relieved the big reveal had gone smoothly, it had taken her a few hours to notice the change. But it was definitely there. And it was glaringly obvious he *loved* playing the part of dad. The way he looked at Lulah made her ovaries sing. But would that last?

Gunnar stroked a hand along her thigh. "Nervous?"

"A little."

"Mom and Dad are going to love you, and you've already met Axel."

Her stomach kicked wildly at the mention of his parents. Gunnar might be convinced they'd love her, but she knew better. Would they judge her? Think she was a slut for seducing her son? Worse, would they treat Lulah differently? She found it hard to take a deep breath.

"Hey." Gunnar stroked her cheek with the back of a finger, pulling her out of her maudlin imaginings. "I promise, they're going to love both of you." He hopped out of the truck, and jogged around the front to open her door. He gave her hand an extra squeeze as he helped her down. "Stay there while I help Lulah out of her car seat." He pushed the passenger seat forward, and after fiddling with the straps, lifted Lulah out and settled her on his hip. "Wanna walk, baby girl?" She shook her head, burying it in his neck.

Suzannah was stunned at how their relationship had changed over the course of the day. It was like her little heart had been waiting for him. A pang of guilt pulled at her. Maybe she should have looked for him when she discovered she was pregnant. She shook herself. She'd done her best, and what was important, was that he was here now. Gunnar took her hand, lacing his fingers through hers, and led her from the parking area down around the back of the house to where they'd spread out picnic tables covered in festive tablecloths under the shade of two large oak trees. Someone had strung red, white, and blue paper lanterns between the branches. At the edges, several tiki torches had been lit, even though it was early afternoon. She caught a whiff of citronella. Suzannah couldn't help but smile, the scene was the quintessential country picnic, straight out of Pinterest or Country Living.

Gunnar called out as they approached. "Ma, Pops, come meet Suzannah."

She could hear the pride in his voice, especially when they approached and he tilted his head to Lulah, who clung to him.

"Meet my best girl." She hardly recognized his voice through the emotion. "'Zannah, this is my mom and dad."

She extended her hand. "It's a real pleasure, Mr. and Mrs. Hansen. Gunnar's told me so much about you both."

Martha wrapped her in a soft embrace. "Hush, now. You call me Martha. And you can just call Eddie Pops. And who is this?" She lowered her voice, giving Lulah a pat on the back. "Hi there, honey. You can just call me Besta – that's what all the kids call me. And this guy is Bumpa." Lulah snuggled deeper into Gunnar, offering a shy smile.

Martha turned to her. "Is Lulah short for something?"

Huh. Funny Gunnar hadn't told her. "Yes," she answered, stomach fluttering. "It's short for Talulah Belle."

Martha's eyes went wide, and her eyes grew misty.

"Talulah for my grandmother."

"And my middle name is Belle," Martha said, stunned.

Suzannah nodded, tears poking at her eyeballs. Even through her heartache, she'd wanted to make sure her baby knew where she'd come from, and to have some kind of tie to Gunnar's family.

Martha blinked, wrapping her in another hug. "You have no idea what that means to me. Thank you," she whispered. She stepped back, swiping her face with the back of her hand. "Now I've gone and gotten all emotional. Who'd like some lemonade?"

Gunnar placed a hand at the small of her back. "I'm gonna introduce you around, but don't worry about remembering everyone's names. There's a bunch of us." In short order, Gunnar introduced her to his entire family.

Axel, whom she remembered, and who welcomed her with a bearhug, and his wife Haley, and their little baby Melody, who was still in a sling.

Hope, their sister, and her husband, Ben Sinclaire. His family lived across the river and shared a property line.

Their cousin Maddie and her husband Blake, Ben's older brother. They had a son, Henry, who was toddling around and hiding underneath the furniture.

Blake and Ben's brother, Brodie, brought his wife, Jamey, who Gunnar mentioned had helped Martha prepare most of the spread.

Lastly, Gunnar's Aunt Peggy, his cousin Parker's mom, and her boyfriend Zack Forte, who used to be Haley's boss.

Yep. No way in a month of Sundays, would Suzannah remember everyone. Or how they were connected.

Martha offered her a glass of lemonade, and a smile. "Do you feel thoroughly intimidated, now?"

"Pretty much. Although Maddie brought Henry in for a physical." Suzannah took a long sip of the sweet-tart, obviously made from scratch, beverage.

"Everyone seems thrilled there's finally a doctor in town."

"To be honest, I'm surprised at how busy we've been."

"Do you think you need help?"

Suzannah wasn't sure how to answer. Half the Hansens and Sinclaires were on the board. Anything she said was likely to get back to the other members, and she didn't want to come across as whiny, or incompetent. "Having someone sit at the receptionist's desk has been really helpful." She paused, debating whether to say more. "I think many people have put off seeking medical care for a very long time. It's natural that when you finally have a doctor, that there'd be a backlog of visits."

Martha nodded quietly. "Let us know if it becomes something different. I know it's a lot for one person to handle."

Nothing she couldn't handle though. She couldn't

afford to give the board any indication she wasn't able to fulfill the duties of the job. Even if she thought they were a bit unreasonable. Just the other day, she'd had to send a family to Manhattan because the child had a compound fracture in his arm and needed surgery. There was no x-ray machine here, not to mention she didn't know the first thing about taking x-rays, and she could only detect the most basic issues on x-ray film. She was a doctor, not an x-ray tech or a radiologist. Helping the family come to terms with the reality they *still* were going to have to drive over an hour for medical care, had been… challenging.

"Can I ask you a question?" Martha asked.

"Sure. Anything."

"Would you consider… would it be alright if we helped with Lulah? If you're not comfortable bringing her out here, I could come into town. Gunnar told us about her heart and everything she's been through." Martha took her hand, gripping it hard. "I-I just want you to know, we consider you family. We're here for you no matter what."

Warmth flooded Suzannah. "I… thank you," she said, overwhelmed. "That's so kind of you." She was unused to such kindness from strangers, and yet… it felt really nice.

Gunnar appeared at her side, hand coming to rest at the small of her back. His touch warmed her straight to her toes. "I thought maybe we'd take a little ride before eating?" He gave her a knowing smile. "And don't worry about the heat. Nothing out on the table has mayonnaise. All the perishable food is inside where it's cool."

"Did I have that look?"

He grinned down at her. "The one that says you're worried about treating a full-blown food poisoning epidemic? Yeah." He raised his eyebrows and motioned over to a set of lawn chairs set up by the tree. "You see Lulah trying to play with Henry? She's trying to get him to play Batman, and he's having none of it." Laughter dripped from his voice. "He just wants to dig in the dirt."

"Well, let's rescue them both. I bet Lulah will be thrilled."

"What about you?"

"More nervous than thrilled. But I'll get used to it. I trust you." The last words popped out before she could censor them. But it was true – she trusted him. At least when it came to horses.

"Yeah?" His eyes bored into her.

She nodded, mouth suddenly like sawdust. "Yeah." The air between them grew heavy, and the noise from the gathering faded away.

Gunnar spoke low, so only she could hear. "Sometimes, you get this look in your eye, and I just want to kiss you."

Her heart jumped into her throat, then dropped to her toes, leaving her limbs tingling. She opened her mouth to speak, but no sound came out, and honestly, what could she say? Because she wanted him to kiss her. More than anything. And truth be told, it was becoming harder and harder to hold him at arm's length. At last, she dragged her eyes from his. "Lulah," she called, working to bring her voice to heel. "Would you like to go see the horses?"

Lulah immediately jumped up from where Henry was seated, and ran to them. Gunnar scooped her up and placed her on his shoulders, her favorite place. "Now, hold onto my hat. Don't let the wind blow it away," he instructed as they started for the barn. "If you have fun today, I'll get you your own hat and boots."

"Will they be Batman boots?"

Suzannah let out a belly laugh. Gunnar followed suit. "I'll see what we can find, Lulahbug. I'll see what we can find."

The door to the barn stood open, and together, they

entered the dim space. The scent of hay and fresh manure hit her nose, but surprisingly, it wasn't offensive. As they slowly walked down the aisle, she picked up the scent of leather, horse, and fresh cedar. In all, a comforting, outdoorsy, earthy aroma that slowed her heart rate with each breath.

Gunnar stopped in front of a beautiful Palomino, and spoke in hushed tones. "So, Lulahbug. When we're in the barn, we always talk quiet. We don't want to scare the horses."

"She's pretty," Lulah answered with quiet reverence.

"Would you like to pet her nose? This is Lucy. She's one of the gentlest horses we own."

Gunnar stepped sideways to allow Lulah's outstretched hand reach the horse's nose. She touched it, then immediately pulled back with a giggle. "It's fuzzy."

"It is."

Gunnar walked a little further. "This is Fleur. You and I are going to ride her. She's also very gentle." He shot Suzannah a reassuring look. "Normally, I ride Buzz, one of our stallions. But Fleur could use the exercise, and she's really great with kids."

Fear clutched at Suzannah. "You're not going to let her ride alone are you?"

Gunnar shook his head. "No way. She'll ride with me." He put Lulah down. "If you walk a bit farther down the aisle, there's a stack of hay bales. Take a seat there, and I'll bring the horses out to saddle. You can watch."

Taking Lulah's tiny hand, they found the hay bales and watched in rapt attention while Gunnar saddled both horses, talking to them about what he was doing the whole time.

"Is it okay I don't have boots?"

Gunnar nodded. "Sure. And if you like it enough to go

out again, I'll outfit you both with boots." He led the horses out of the barn, then returned, motioning them to follow. "We have to let the horses stand and walk a bit before we mount up. They like to swell their bellies at first, and we need to re-check the cinch to make sure it's tight enough." They re-entered the hot afternoon sun, and Gunnar stopped, holding out an arm. "A couple of rules around horses. Always mount from the left, and avoid getting too close to their backsides. Can you remember that?"

A tremor of fear shook Suzannah as she nodded. Was this really a good idea, riding horses? They were so big. A fall from the saddle could result in broken arms, torn ligaments, even head injury. She shuddered, ready to turn back around.

Gunnar's hand was at her back in an instant. "Take it easy, doc. Nothing bad's gonna happen. These are the gentlest, most seasoned horses in the stable."

"That obvious, huh?" She laughed sheepishly.

He angled his body away from Lulah and nuzzled her neck. "I'd never let either of you get hurt. I promise."

His mouth against her skin sent fingers of awareness tingling through her, but before she could chastise him for being too expressive in front of Lulah, he stepped back, giving her a little wink. Devil, he was teasing her, and she rather liked it. Swinging Lulah up, he set her on the saddle. "Hold on to this with both hands, okay? I'm gonna help your mama, and then I'm going to mount up behind you."

"It's like the merry-go-round, mama." Her eyes were wide with wonder.

"You mean the carousel? Yes, I guess it is."

Gunnar led her to Lucy, and placed his hands on her hips. But his touch felt more like a caress than help. Heat radiated off him, warming her back, and it took all her self-control to keep from snuggling into him. He chuckled quietly in her ear. "Do you know how hard it is for me to keep my hands off you right now?"

"Then don't," she answered boldly. "I want your hands on me in the worst way."

He pressed into her, squeezing her hips tighter. A shiver of pure wanton desire rippled down her spine, tightening her nipples and settling deep in her core. His voice, when he spoke, came out like gravel. "We're gonna clear the air later, just you and me. Understand?"

A thrill of anticipation shot through her. She was ready. In fact, she couldn't wait. She nodded, not trusting her voice.

"Okay," he continued quietly, but loud enough for Lulah to hear. "Place your foot in the stirrup, and on three, I want you to push off, then swing your right leg over the saddle. I'll give you a boost." He counted, and the next thing she knew, she was up and settling herself in the saddle, but not before he'd given her ass an intimate caress.

In a flash, Gunnar settled himself behind Lulah, reins in one hand, arm securely wrapped around her torso. Suzannah's breath lodged in her throat, heart expanding. They both beamed, Lulah barely able to contain her excitement, a look of complete satisfaction on Gunnar's face. And damn if he wasn't sexy as sin holding their child. Suzannah's lady parts flooded with heat. *DILF*, indeed.

"Wait." She called, reaching into her back pocket for her phone. "I have to take a picture." Lulah's smile stretched until her eyes became squinty. She snapped several pictures before putting it away. "I'll text them to you."

Gunnar locked eyes with her, and she felt the pull between them, powerfully. A charge of anticipation surged through her. Yes, they definitely needed to talk later.

Chapter Seventeen

"You've got the look of a hungry man, my brother," Axel ribbed as he handed Gunnar an ice-cold beer. "So what's the deal between you two, anyway?" Axel nodded to where Suzannah, Maddie, and Haley all sat under the shade of one of the trees.

"You don't pull your punches, do you?"

"Never have, never will."

"Glad to see marriage hasn't changed you."

Axel grinned. "Oh, it has. But I'm still an asshole." He took a draw from the longneck he held.

Gunnar laughed outright, even as a place in his chest pulled tight. "Damn, it's just not the same without you here every day."

"Are you saying you miss me, big brother?"

"Nope. Not at all." His mouth quirked as he grabbed a long sip. "I enjoy not having to look over my shoulder at every turn, worried I'm gonna run into one of your pranks."

Axel gave him a sly look. "Maybe I left a few for you to discover."

"Nice try, asshole. I scoured this place from top to bottom when you left."

This time Axel let out a belly laugh. "You know I had to try."

Gunnar grew serious. "Do you think you'll move back at some point?"

"Haley's happy as a pig in mud, and I'm getting clients. I miss the ranch, but we've got a pretty sweet setup at home."

Home. The way Axel said 'home', made him ache. No doubt about it, Axel was never moving back to this home. Gunnar clapped him on the back. "I'm happy for you, man."

"You given any more thought to hiring a foreman?"

Gunnar shook his head. "Pops wasn't too keen when I brought it up. Wants to keep everything in the family."

Axel shook his head, cursing under his breath. "I thought the heart attack might have jolted some perspective into him."

"Oh, it did. He's softer. But he's a Hansen, so still stubborn as fuck."

Axel snorted. "Got that right." He toed the grass beneath his boots. "But I have to say, you look like hell. I'm glad to see you embracing fatherhood and all, but you're working way too hard. You don't want to end up like dad. Or Uncle Warren."

"I've got a long way to go before I have to worry about that."

Axel looked skeptical. "I don't know, man. You're under way more stress than Pops. Pops ran the ranch with Uncle Warren and all of us. And things were... easier then. Look, don't let Pops guilt you into doing something that's not good for you. Or her." He gestured to Lulah. "You've gotta think about your little girl now."

"And I want this to be her legacy," Gunnar said fiercely. "I'm not giving that up. We're in the black right now, between leasing some acreage to the Sinclaires for grazing, and the money that comes in from the paintball course. Emma Sinclaire has taken over the marketing for that, and we're booked two months out now. All these corporate groups come out for team building."

Axel took his shoulder. "Great. I'm thrilled for you. All I'm saying is that you may find you need to adjust your priorities."

"I can do both. Hell, I've been doing both. I've been going over every night for dinner since I found out."

Axel gave him a hard stare. "There's a lot more to parenting than just dinner. Don't forget that."

Someone started a bonfire after dinner, the flames shooting high into the twilight as family and friends scattered across the lawn. The Sinclaires' half-brother, Simon, now a freshman in high school, had invited a few friends over, and were picking through songs on an old beat-up guitar someone had found. Dottie Grace and her husband Teddy had joined Martha and Eddie on the porch, watching over the festivities like ancient royalty. Suzannah and Maddie stepped off the porch together, having just come from inside where they'd put Lulah and Henry to sleep in the guest bedroom.

Gunnar rose from his lawn chair at the edge of the bonfire. Maybe now he could grab a few minutes alone with Suzannah. He intercepted her as she crossed the lawn. "Lulah settled?"

She answered with a tender smile. "She and Henry fell right to sleep, holding hands. I thought I was going to melt."

That did sound pretty adorable. "Have you had fun this afternoon?"

"I have. Your family is pretty wonderful." Her face contorted, and she looked away.

Instantly, he was on high alert. "What? What is it? Was someone a dick? I swear, I'll—"

She held up her hand. "Stop. I've had a great time today. And Lulah, too. For a second, it made me realize how much my family's missed out on."

"I don't understand." And shit, now she looked downcast.

"It's nothing. Really. And I don't want to ruin this perfect day with thoughts of my crazy family."

Now his curiosity was peaked. "Let's go on a walk, we can talk."

"No, really. It's okay."

Gunnar grabbed her hand. "First, I don't like to see you upset. Second, I was hoping to get you alone anyway. Third, no one will miss us."

"Are you sure?" Her voice was filled with doubt.

"Positive. Look around. The teenagers have taken over. My folks and the Graces are keeping an eye on them. Everyone else has pretty much scattered." Gunnar had his own ideas about why that was, but for now, he wanted to go sit someplace quiet, talk a little, and canoodle a whole lot more. "I grabbed a blanket from the truck, which direction do you want to go?"

"But what about Lulah? What if she wakes up?"

"My folks will be there. And Dottie's there too," he cajoled. "She'll be fine." Suzannah might still be leery of his folks, but she trusted Dottie. He gave her hand a gentle tug. "Please?"

She softened, finally nodding. "Okay."

Gunnar gave a silent little fist pump, and led her to where he'd stashed the blanket. Tucking it under one arm, he skirted the bonfire and cut between the farmhouse and the barn, heading north toward one of the hills that dotted their property. The first stars winked to life as the sky melted to mauve, then indigo.

A fire burned brightly in Gunnar's chest as they hiked over dips and crannies he could traverse with his eyes shut. Suzannah's breath became labored as they scaled the last hill to where a lone oak stood like a queen surveying her realm. "Need a rest?"

"I'm good. Just a little out of shape."

Her admission surprised him. "How is it doctors can be out of shape?"

She laughed, a bright, melodious sound that heated his insides. "Let's start with the long hours, and higher levels of cortisol from stress and sleep deprivation. It helps that I'm on my feet nearly all day, but that's different than going for a jog or hitting the weights."

"And you probably don't eat so well."

"You noticed?"

"I'm worried the board has asked too much of you," he conceded.

"This is so much better than my residency. I'm fine. Really," she added when he narrowed his eyes.

Gunnar spread the blanket just below the crest of the hill. He preferred to have an unobstructed view of the stars. Dropping to the blanket, he patted the ground between his legs. She sank down, not resisting when he wrapped his arms around her and pulled her against his chest. A light breeze danced up from the south carrying with it, the scent of warm earth and dewy grass. In the distance, a coyote yipped, and the tree frogs began to sing. Fireflies rose up, winking around them as the sky faded to black. For a long time, neither of them spoke. "This is the place I wanted to bring you to. Before," he murmured, placing his chin on top of her head.

"It's beautiful."

"Magic of the Flint Hills. Sometimes it feels like a place out of time. Especially on a quiet night like this, where I can almost imagine our ancestors coming by covered wagon."

"When did your family arrive here?"

"Eighteen-fifties. Not long after the Sinclaires settled across the creek."

A thoughtful hum emanated from her throat, as if she was thinking deeply.

He continued, struggling to put his thoughts into adequate words. "I always wanted my children to grow up tied to this land. Six generations of Hansens have poured their lifeblood into this acreage. We've survived floods, droughts, storms, war, and depression. This land has kept us alive. Given us everything. We... *I* can't let it go. You know, my uncle Warren's ashes are scattered underneath that tree."

"That one, there?"

"Mmm-hmm."

Her body pulled inward, tensing. "I-I'd never ask you to give this up."

"But?"

She shook her head. "There's no caveat. This land is who you are. Anyone with half a brain can see it. You're as rooted to the soil as that tree." She twisted, pointing to the tree. Her skin glowed in the starlight, ethereal and other-worldly. As if she were a luminous Tallemaja or an elvish creature from the Swedish fairytales of his childhood, fair and beautiful.

"You turn me inside out, 'Zannah," he rasped, bringing a hand to her cheek. "I forget which way is up with you." He stroked a thumb over her satin skin. "I never stopped loving you, deep down."

She froze, eyes wide. Silence loomed over them. For a moment, even the frogs went quiet.

"Did I say too much?" His voice came out barely a whisper, because saying it, admitting it, would surely make it so.

Her hand dropped to his shoulder and the next thing he knew, they were kissing with reckless abandon. Desperately, as if it was their last kiss. Or their first kiss in too long. He tangled his fingers in her silky hair, pulling it free from her signature ponytail, deepening their connection, sliding his tongue across hers, plundering and tasting.

She shifted her hips around, and together they tumbled to the ground, a tangle of limbs. He rolled, so his hips pinned hers, notching his erection against her pussy, and braced his arms alongside her head. She stared up at him, eyes bright pools in the darkness. "So beautiful," he murmured, dropping a kiss at her temple. "So soft." He trailed kisses along her cheekbone. "Be with me, 'Zannah. Let me be your man."

She whimpered as he took her mouth again, pouring all his feeling into their connection.

"Yes, oh yes, Gunnar," she murmured when he pulled away. "There's never been anyone but you."

At her words, a weight lifted off his chest. Warmth flooded him. Light. They came together, limbs colliding in an effort to quickly remove clothing. Boots toed off, shirts yanked over heads, pants shimmied down, until they were panting and naked, clothing strewn across the blanket like a mini-explosion had gone off.

Gunnar sat back on his heels, cock jutting out, thick and heavy, and stared unabashedly. Fucking gorgeous. She was rounder, more voluptuous than before, body stretched from carrying his child. Hips full, belly soft, breasts heavy. All plusses in his book. Changes borne out of love. He reached for her ankle, and kissed the hollow inside her ankle bone. "You're perfection, 'Zannah."

He marked a trail up the inside of her leg, branding her with his mouth. Pausing at the sensitive spots he remembered, kissing those places until she moaned, or twitched, or both. He aimed to feast on her fully, until her cries of ecstasy echoed off the hills. "Open for me, sweetheart," he said, stroking the inside of her thighs. "Let me give it to you like I know you like it."

Suzannah opened wider with a sigh, staring at him through heavy-lidded eyes, mouth parted.

"Do you know how beautiful you are?" His voice was a husk. "I'm gonna make you feel so good."

"Oh yes, please." She gave him a loopy smile. "I love what you do to me."

He bent, inhaling her essence, delighting as she cried out when his tongue split her wet folds. Something deep inside him slid home as her taste hit his brain. He licked at her like a man dying of thirst. And maybe he had been, without her. But the drought was over now, and he meant to take his fill. Her hips rose to meet him, as he drew her clit into his mouth, sucking the aroused bead. He nearly came when he fucked her hot channel, and she squeezed around his tongue, filling his mouth with her glorious musky sweet taste. Her hips rolled in a time of her own making, but he picked up on it, and matched her tempo, lick, thrust, suck. Lick, thrust, suck, until at last, she let go with a high wail that shook him to his bones.

He reached for his pants, rooting until he found the condom he'd jammed in his pocket at the last minute, just in case. Sheathing himself, he sank into her while she was still shaking like a leaf in the aftermath of her orgasm. His eyes nearly rolled into his skull from the tight heat of her. This wasn't some meaningless coupling, a mindless fuck purely for release. This was fucking church, and he was praying at the altar of Suzannah, the only woman he'd ever given himself to – body, mind, and soul. This was a homecoming as sweet and poignant as the prodigal son. A gift to be cherished, fiercely protected.

He curled over her, bending to press a kiss between her ample breasts. He took a mouthful, swirling his tongue over a rosy peak. Slowly rocking into her, making sure he dragged his cock across her swollen clit as they moved together in a rhythm as old as these hills. She loved it slow, loved his deep thrusts, and he took his time, arms straining from the effort of holding back, but he could feel her orgasm building. Winding through her body, coiling tight, ready to snap.

The back of his legs burned, the ache to release building with each slow thrust. Another moment and they'd be launched into the stratosphere. She ground into him, breathing hot and heavy, moans mingling with her outbreath, until her eyes flew open wide, and she half gasped, half cried, as her pussy clenched around him, contracting with such intensity, he followed her over the cliff with a loud cry. Cries turned to laughter as joyous thrusts continued, both of them riding the ecstatic wave into nothingness. With a final thrust and groan, Gunnar dropped his head. Planting a kiss at Suzannah's temple, then at the hollow in her neck, letting out a sigh of complete satisfaction.

She raised her head and nipped at his collarbone, then licked the hollow at the base of his neck, before dropping her head back to the ground. Neither of them spoke. The moment felt too holy, too sacred. As if some kind of sacred bond had been forged with the heat of their bodies.

Too soon, he rolled off her to dispose of the condom, but in the next breath, he was back, wrapping her into his arms as the night sounds settled over them like a blanket. A sliver of a moon continued its march toward the horizon. Suzannah rolled over, propping herself on an elbow. "Just so we're clear. What does it mean to be my man?"

He had to smile. Leave it to her mind to catch hold of that phrase and define it. He shrugged. "Not dating other people?"

"No brainer." A frown tugged at the corner of her mouth. "What else?"

His heart pounded. "I think we should move in together. Be a family."

"Oh."

Fuck. She sounded disappointed. He should have waited, given her more time to get used to the idea.

"But where would we live?"

A tendril of worry snaked through him. There was no way he could move into town. No way he'd consider it. Not with his responsibilities here. But he didn't want to disappoint her either. "Here," he said, drawing out the word. "Then ma and pops could help with Lulah. And my day starts pretty early. Four-thirty most days."

"But what about my job?"

"It's only twenty minutes."

"You and Lulah could drive in together. Or, she could quit preschool and stay on the ranch, like we all did."

"She's *not* quitting Montessori," Suzannah said sharply, sitting up and reaching for her clothes.

"Okay, okay. It was just an idea."

"And what if there's an emergency? I'm supposed to be on call. How can I be on call if I'm twenty minutes away?" Fuck. He hadn't even thought of that. The board would have his head if she moved out to the ranch. The whole reason the Graces donated the bungalow across from the clinic was so that the doctor could be on call for emergencies. But there was no way he was moving into town. He couldn't. Who would run the ranch?

Suzannah continued. "I think it would be a big adjustment for Lulah. She only just found out you're her dad."

Disappointment crashed through him. He'd bungled this in every possible way. She was right. It was too soon, and he *hated* that.

She dropped a hand to his shoulder. "I'm sorry Gunnar. Can we table that possibility until later? Maybe see how things go for a little bit? You could still come for dinner every night."

This sucked. He felt like second runner-up at a beauty pageant. But the pragmatic part of him knew it made sense.

He assented, defeat settling over him like a wet blanket. "You should plan on Sunday dinners over here."

"I'd like that. Very much. I think Lulah would like it too."

Suzannah burrowed into his chest again and instinctively, his arms came around her. He would not give into despair. This was just a bump in the road. Okay, maybe a sinkhole. But they could figure it out, couldn't they? She wouldn't shut him out a second time, would she?

Chapter Eighteen

_____

*S*uzannah crept into Lulah's bedroom, bathed in the soft glow of morning sunshine filtered through curtains. For a moment, her heart stopped, too full of joy and love. Her precious baby had made it to four. And so far, knock on wood, her heart valves seemed to be in good shape. Lulah's blonde mop spread across her pillow, chubby cheeks soft as she cooed in her sleep. She couldn't imagine loving Lulah more than she did right now.

Dropping to her knees beside the little bed, she drew a finger across her still baby-soft cheek. "Good morning Lulahbelle. Time to wake up. Do you know what today it?"

Her eyes fluttered open and she blinked the sleep away, slowly coming to. Suzannah nearly laughed outloud at the moment her brain woke up. The change in Lulah was instantaneous. A wide smile puffed out her cheeks. "It's my birday."

Suzannah didn't think it was possible to be more in love with this child. *Birday.* Lulah still had trouble making some of her sounds. Not a cause for worry, yet. And in the meantime, it was so stinking cute. "That's right. And how old are you today?"

"I'm *FOUR*." Her voice rose in excitement.

"And do you remember what we're going to do today?"

"We're going out to my, to..." she hesitated, looking confused.

Suzannah's heart twisted. She should have dealt with this a month ago, but she hadn't been sure how to handle it, and she didn't want to force anything on Lulah. "That's right, we're going out to Gunnar's. To your daddy's." She took a fortifying breath. "Lulahbug, sweetie, it's okay to call him daddy if you want. You can call him whatever you like."

Lulah grew very solemn. "Dylan's mommy and daddy don't live together, but he still calls him Daddy."

"I don't think Gunnar would mind if you called him daddy." She was pretty sure he'd be over the moon.

"Would that make him live with us?"

The question acted like a bomb. Suzannah froze, heart sinking. She'd been dreading this question more than any other. Simple answer. Lulah had asked a simple, under-standable, four-year-old question. The worst thing she could do was over complicate it. Four-year-olds dealt with concrete realities, not abstract ones. "Do you want Gunnar – your daddy – to live with us?"

Lulah looked ready to cry as she nodded.

Gunnar would be thrilled. As it was, he spent most evenings with them, leaving after he'd helped put Lulah to bed. They'd become experts in sneaky sex, but he'd never spent the night. Often, he had to be in bed not long after Lulah, and she couldn't justify asking him to stay at the bungalow when she refused to stay at the ranch. It didn't seem fair to expect him to make all the sacrifices. Espe-cially since he gave them so much already. She hadn't had to cook dinner once since he'd re-entered their lives. As good a gift as any in her book.

Her paperwork had slid since Gunnar had taken up their evenings, and now most nights, she was up until two or three in the morning, sometimes later, working to stay on top of the massive amount of paperwork the clinic generated. It was exhausting, but she didn't see how either of them could get off the merry-go-round they were riding.

"Aww, honey." Suzannah gathered her sweet baby into her arms, heart pounding with trepidation. Life just became exponentially more complicated. "You love your daddy, don't you?"

Lulah nodded into her shoulder.

"I think you should tell him that, because I know he loves you, too, bug. And in the meantime, I have a surprise for you."

That seemed to put the sparkle back into her eyes. "Special breakfast?"

"Even better, c'mon." She pulled Lulah into her arms and struggled to stand. "I think you grew overnight, I can hardly hold you anymore." Suzannah knew that day was fast approaching, when Lulah would be too big to carry. And while she loved that her baby was strong and healthy enough, and *big* enough to stand on her own two feet, the prospect of no longer carrying her baby was bittersweet.

Lulah giggled and wiggled out of her embrace. "I'm a big girl, mama," she said proudly, and ran out of the room, squealing with delight when she encountered the visitors waiting for her. Iris and Bailey had driven in this morning, and Iris was already at work in the kitchen making blueberry cardamom pancakes.

Bailey handed her a mimosa when she entered the

kitchen. "Happy birthday, mama. You need to be celebrated, too. And pampered. Have a seat."

Suzannah dropped into a chair, pushing a streamer out of the way. The aunties had pulled out all the stops, packing their car with streamers and balloons, party hats and pretty paper napkins. Suzannah loved them for it. Lulah stood at the stove, helping Iris. "Be careful," she called out.

"I *told* you, I'm a big girl mommy."

"Stop helicoptering, mama." Iris giggled. "It's not like I work with six and seven-year-olds every day."

"You need to relax." Bailey stared at her hard. "You're working too much."

Oh, no. Suzannah had been worried about this when they'd called to say they were coming. She lifted a shoulder, brushing off Bailey's concern. "I'm a practice of one. I knew it would be long hours." Not this long, though. She'd foolishly assumed they'd hired admin and billing help before she arrived. And she hadn't expected her weekends on call to be so busy. Technically, the clinic was closed on the weekends, but she was on call for urgent care, and some Saturdays urgent care lasted all day. Fortunately, on those busy days, she'd been able to hire Ms. Annie or Ms. Ivy from the Montessori school to babysit Lulah at the last minute. But she'd always worried about what would happen if they both were busy.

Bailey scoffed. "This isn't Northern Exposure. They can't work you to the bone like this. It's unethical."

That got her hackles up. "We're all doing the best we can out here, Bailes. I've never seen a community of people who work so hard. Half the ranchers here have second and third jobs. Most of the fire department is *volunteer*. Everyone pitches in to help out. I'm not going to turn my back on them when they need me."

Bailey's dark eyes flashed. "Fair enough. But they also need you to be healthy, too. Have you looked in the mirror lately? Your skin is sallow, you've got bags under your eyes, and you've easily lost ten pounds."

"That's just baby weight coming off."

Bailey choked on her mimosa. "I call BS," she said. "Your baby is four."

Okay, so maybe she'd skipped too many meals, but she was used to powering through on adrenaline and coffee. It's what all doctors did, right?

"Enough shop talk over there," Iris called from the stove. "We've got one Birthday-Girl-Breakfast coming up. Miss Lulah? Will you carry the bacon to the table?"

"I don't know how you manage to work your magic, Iris. This is heavenly." In addition to blueberry cardamom pancakes with whipped cream, she'd made sweet potato fries sprinkled with cinnamon and cloves, and piles of bacon.

She smiled enigmatically. "My mother taught me well."

Iris's mother, Parvati, was the best cook Suzannah had ever met, and the woman could cook for a crowd like nobody's business.

Suzannah raised her glass. "Well, lucky us."

"Lucky Lulah," Bailey chimed in. "Lulahbelle, do you know you have the best mommy in the world?"

"And the best daddy," Lulah added.

Her heart sisters exchanged glances. Crap. Now was not the time to bring up Gunnar. "Yes, sweetie. And the best daddy." She gave Iris and Bailey one of those *not now* looks. After breakfast came presents. In addition to books and art supplies, Bailey and Iris had found the cutest Batman tutu that sent Lulah over the moon. "Go put it on," Suzannah encouraged, knowing that after she showed them what it looked like, Lulah would abandon them for make-believe in the living room, and they could talk.

As soon as they could hear Lulah playing pretend in the other room, Bailey poured another round of mimosas. The third degree was about to start. "So. I want details."

"What's really going on here, Suze?" added Iris, giving her *the teacher look*.

"Clearly our girl has been getting some," Bailey waved her glass.

It was pointless to deny. Already the flush was creeping up her neck. "That obvious?" She gave them a sheepish smile.

"The hickie on your collarbone is a dead giveaway."

"*What?*" she squealed, pulling up her pajama shirt. "Do you think Lulah saw?"

"I'd worry more about other people seeing," said Iris, giggling uncontrollably.

"Ohmygod that's *so* junior high."

"Don't worry, if you wear a regular tee-shirt or a collared shirt, no one will notice. Just no cleavage bearing V-necks, 'kay?" Bailey winked.

Like she wore those kinds of shirts anyway, not with her boobs. "Okay, okay, so we might be seeing where things go."

"Does Lulah know?" Iris asked.

"That we're sleeping together?" Suzannah shook her head. "No. Gunnar comes for dinner every night, and we go for Sunday dinner with his family."

Bailey's jaw dropped. "*That's it?* That's the extent of his relationship with her? Dinner?" She clamped her lips together, shaking her head. "Girl, you gotta think about the message you are sending your daughter."

Suzannah's belly tightened. "What do you mean?"

"Is he paying you child support?"

"What about helping with childcare?"

"Is he paying for groceries?"

"Or clothes?"

The questions came rapid-fire from both of them. She could hardly keep up. "He usually brings dinner, or cooks it. And yes, he stocks the fridge. I haven't gone to the grocery store in weeks. And he keeps me in coffee."

Iris rolled her eyes, looking straight at Bailey. "He keeps her in coffee." Sarcasm dripped from her voice. *"And—"* She held up a hand to keep Suzannah from interrupting. "He's got booty on call twenty-four-seven."

Suzannah's face burned. When they put it that way, he sounded awful. "It's not like that," she denied softly. "We both agreed—"

"Agreed on what?" Bailey snapped. "That you could be fuckbuddies? And that you'd bear the brunt of the parenting? You know you could sue him for four years of child support?"

"And help with your medical bills?" added Iris pointedly. "You can*not* keep bearing the burden of raising Lulah by yourself. It's not right."

Hot tears pricked at her eyes. "But he loves her," she said.

"Does he? Does he really?" Bailey's tone of voice said he didn't. "Because, I don't know. If he really loved her, maybe he'd step it up a bit more."

"It sounds like he likes the idea of being a parent more than the reality."

Their words crushed her. They were so right. She'd built up in her mind that their relationship was fair. And that it worked. But looking at the situation through their eyes, she could see the message she was giving Lulah was that everything was on her, the mom. Dads just got to have fun.

Iris grabbed her hand. "Honey, don't beat yourself up. You probably didn't even realize you were doing it. I mean, look at your upbringing. You were raised believing a woman's only role is to serve their husband."

Suzannah sniffed loudly, unable to prevent a tear from leaking out the corner of her eye. "I thought I'd escaped all that. Honest."

"You used your inheritance from Talulah to help with Lulah's medical bills. That money was supposed to set you up in life. And because you don't have it, now you're here – working yourself nearly to death."

"But I never would have reconnected with Gunnar had I not come here."

"Ironic, isn't it?" Bailey came around the table to give her a hug. "And I can see this is tearing you up. But you have got to look at this rationally. Financially."

Iris nodded vigorously. "I'm with Bailey. If he wants the goodies, he needs to step up with the goods."

"But it's not like that. He asked us to move in with him, and I said no."

Both their mouths dropped open. "*Why?*" asked Iris.

"Because it's complicated," snapped Suzannah. "He can't leave the ranch, and I need to be close to the clinic."

Her friends looked dubious.

"And Lulah. I didn't think it was right for us to move in right away. Not when we've just gotten settled." They'd feel differently once they met his family. She was sure of it. "Come to the ranch today. Meet his family. They're good people. Gunnar's parents, Martha and Eddie, dote on Lulah."

Iris gave her the stink-eye. "But have they ever offered to help babysit?"

"Yes," she answered a little too defensively. "Martha

and Eddie have been fantastic. They came to take Lulah to breakfast last Saturday."

"Oh whoop-de-doo." Bailey swirled her finger in the air.

"Stop it. You don't understand. Martha and Eddie still put a full day in on the ranch, Gunnar even more. Everyone's got their hands full." She understood her friends' concern. She'd be equally protective if it were one of them. But they hadn't seen Gunnar with Lulah, how he looked at her. More importantly, how he treated her like she was the most precious person on the planet.

"So how did they do it?"

"Raise kids?" Suzannah shrugged. "They didn't go to preschool. They helped on the ranch from the time they were little until they started school, and then helped before and after. Pretty much every ranching family in the area does that."

"So why not let Lulah spend a few days on the ranch?" Iris asked pointedly.

"No," she answered vehemently. "No. Way."

"So the real reason you're working yourself to exhaustion isn't because there aren't people to help, it's because you're afraid to let Lulah out of your sight. Afraid the second you turn your back, something's gonna happen." Bailey's words cracked her wide open. Right to her deepest darkest fears. "Isn't it?"

Suzannah hung her head, heat prickling across her skull. She couldn't think straight. Her insides were a jumble of confusion, exhaustion, and insecurity. She kept seeing Lulah as a tiny baby, hooked up to all the tubes and machines in the NICU. She couldn't bear it if something happened to her baby, her life. Finally, she shrugged. "I don't know. Maybe. I'm just so used to going it alone."

Iris patted her back. "I know, honey. But you've never

gone it alone. Until here. And you've always struggled with asking for help, even before you got out from under your parents' thumbs. It's one thing to not ask for help for yourself, but it's not about you anymore. You can't keep going like this. It's not healthy for anyone."

Suzannah covered her face with her hands. "I– I'll talk to Gunnar."

Chapter Nineteen

*S*omething was wrong. Gunnar could see it as soon as Suzannah stepped out of the car with Lulah, girlfriends in tow. But before he could take a closer look and figure out what was going on, Lulah had launched herself into his arms with a shout. "*Daddy!*"

Everything in him seized. Like he'd just swallowed a ghost pepper and had gone into cardiac arrest. Had he heard her right? A lump rose hard and fast in his throat. "Hey there, baby girl. Have you had a fun morning?"

"Auntie Iris made booberry pancakes."

"Blueberry pancakes, huh? Did you save me one?"

She gave him a saucy grin and shook her head. "Nope." She kept her mouth closed, and looked so damn adorable, he had to laugh. A giddy lightness tickled at him.

"Aww," he said arching back in mock sadness. "That's okay, because you know what we have for after lunch?"

"*Birday cake!*" she shouted.

"That's right. With two candles."

"No, silly."

Heaven help him, she was sunshine and smiles. "No? Oh, *that*'s right. It's six candles."

She erupted in giggles, and dang if his heart didn't do a happy dance. That sound... was like manna from heaven. "Noooo. I'm four."

"You're *four*? Really?"

She nodded.

He shook his head vigorously. "I can't believe you're so big. Four? Really?" He let the syllables draw out.

"Did you give me a present?"

His belly shook. "You'll have to wait and see."

"Auntie Bailey and Iris gived me a Batman skirt."

"This one?" He fingered the tulle.

Lulah nodded.

"You look like a perfect birthday princess." He kissed her forehead and set her on the ground. "Besta and Bumpa are waiting for you under the trees, why don't you go say hi?"

She bounced off, running as fast as her legs could carry her. When did kids lose their bounce? It seemed that every moment Lulah made began with a bounce. Something in his chest grabbed at the bittersweetness of it all. He wanted to bottle this moment up and keep it forever.

Turning back to the car, he caught Suzannah staring. Her face a picture of tenderness. Her girlfriends wearing expressions of wide-eyed shock. Flashing them a shameless *I caught you staring* grin, he turned and followed Lulah with more than a little swagger in his step. He loved his little girl and would never be one of those stoic types when it came to expressing his feelings for his children. The thought as it entered his head, nearly stopped him in his tracks. *Children?* As in more than one? Yeah. Maybe. Someday, if he was so lucky. His hand drifted to his front pocket. He had a birthday present for Suzannah, too. The kind he hoped might help convince her he was serious about staying in Lulah's life. And hers too, if she let him.

Maddie had popped over with little Henry, who was bouncing on Eddie's lap looking happy as a horse in clover. Hope and Ben had joined them too. His sister and cousins both showing baby bumps. Gunnar clapped Ben on the shoulders. "Appreciate you being here and preventing this from becoming a hen party."

Ben chuckled. "My pleasure. Figured I could use the practice."

Gunnar's chest twinged. He'd missed so much. "All you need to remember is Hope's in charge."

"Spoken like a true brother," Ben answered wryly.

When lunch was finished, Gunnar stood and passed out cardboard cone hats. "All right, everyone's got to put one on before we sing Happy Birthday."

Lulah bounced in her seat, eyes shining in hopeful anticipation. He'd fly up and give her the moon if he could. Would she like her gift? More importantly, would her mother? Nervous energy zipped through him as Martha brought out the Batman cake she'd constructed.

Thank you, Suzannah mouthed, eyes full of gratitude.

He pointed at Martha. *All mom*, he mouthed back.

Suzannah made a heart shape with her hands, then dropped them when Bailey gave her a nudge, turning her attention back to Lulah. Gunnar used the opportunity to slip away, and made a beeline for the barn. Once there, he ducked into the first stall. A gray and white Section A Welsh pony lifted her head, training her big dark eye on him. "Hey there, girl." He reached out to give her neck a scratch. "You ready for your big reveal?" Grabbing the halter from its hook, he slipped it over her head. Reaching into his pocket, he pulled out a roll of wide pink satin ribbon, and proceeded to loop it around her neck, tying it in a messy bow. He'd spent all morning brushing the gentle mare until her coat shone and her mane flowed freely. He'd even polished her hooves. She was a pretty little thing, and the perfect horse for a beginning rider. Just to be certain, he'd had Hope spend the afternoon in the round pen with her yesterday. With Hope's stamp of approval, he knew he'd chosen right. Heart galloping in his chest, he led the tiny little pony – just under twelve hands high – up the rise to the birthday table.

Iris saw him first, mouth shaping into an 'oh'. She elbowed Bailey, who in turn, elbowed Suzannah. His breath lodged in his lungs as he waited for her response. Surely she wouldn't say no? She'd seen how much Lulah enjoyed riding with him. She seemed to enjoy their Sunday afternoon outings with Lulah as much as he did. What would she say when the entire surprise came together? Hope and Ben had purchased a pair of pink and red cowboy boots for Lulah, and Maddie had offered to buy a straw cowboy hat. A pair of Ariats for Suzannah sat in a discreet bag at the end of the table, compliments of his parents.

From Maddie's lap, Henry squealed and pointed at the horse. "Hosey," he gurgled, waving a pudgy finger. "Hosey."

His antics captured Lulah's attention who turned, then dropped her fork, eyes flying from the pony to him, once, twice, three times. Suzannah leaned down and said something he couldn't catch. She must have encouraged her, because Lulah scrambled down and ran to the end of the table. She only stopped when Suzannah called out sharply. "What did Gunnar teach you?"

Lulah paused, body vibrating.

Gunnar squatted down. "Come here, baby girl. Would you like to meet your new pony?"

Lulah slowly approached, just like he'd taught her, and held out the back of her hand. The pony's ears pricked forward. "Is she mine?" she asked, hopefulness and doubt mixing in her tiny voice.

"Sure thing. Would you like to name her?"

Lulah broke into a big smile, nodding. "Batman."

"That's a good name, but the pony's a girl."

"Her name's Batman," she answered with determination.

"Alrighty, then. Batman it is. Would you like to get on her back?"

She nodded, and Gunnar lifted her, placing her gently on the pony's back. "Now grab her mane with both hands and I'll walk you in a circle."

"Look, mama," she said with glee, voice rising. "I'm riding all by myself."

"You are. Good for you, bug." Suzannah clapped, looking simultaneously like she was so proud, and at the same time like she'd swallowed a walnut. "You're doing great."

After Gunnar led her around the yard and back down to the barn, he slowed to a stop, Batman right with him. "Okay, princess, time to get down. We'll do some more the next time you're here, okay?"

Lulah leaned out and wrapped her arms around his neck. Two steps back and he planted her on solid ground. "Now we have to put her in the stall." Gunnar led Batman into the barn, Lulah clutching his jeans. He showed Lulah how to take off Batman's harness, where it went on the rack, and how to check her feed and water. "When you're bigger you can do all this by yourself. But in the meantime, you can help me. Does that sound okay?"

"You bet." She nodded emphatically.

"Have you had a nice birthday, kiddo?"

She answered with a heart-melting grin.

Scooping her up and placing her on top of his shoulders, he left the barn. "What do you say, we make sure Mommy got enough ice-cream?"

"Yay," Lulah shouted, clutching his hair. He didn't care it hurt so much his eyes watered. When they returned to the table, Iris and Bailey stood, offering to help Martha with the dishes. In short order, he and Suzannah were alone, under the trees.

"You think they orchestrated this?' he asked, flashing her a quick smile.

"They're like that." A pause. "I love the boots, thank you."

"Do they fit okay?"

"Umm-hmm, perfect. And the pony. I'd say it was too much, except it's perfect for Lulah."

Warmth shot through his body. "Yeah?"

She nodded, smiling. "Every little girl imagines having a pony."

"Even you?"

"Yeah. Even me. Just please promise me, you'll get her a helmet as soon as you stop leading her around?"

"Of course." Another pause. "I have something else for you." He dropped into a lawn chair across from her.

Her brows knit together. "Why's that?"

Gunnar's chest grew tight, unease rising like a giant ball. He dug into his pocket, fishing out the check that had been burning a hole there all day. "Here." He held out the folded paper.

"What's this?" She faltered, taking it only when he thrust it in her direction a second time.

Gunnar inhaled long and slow, gathering his wits. "I went to see our family's lawyer. Nothing to worry about," he rushed, extending a hand to placate her when she sucked in a hard breath. Her eyes bugged out when she unfolded the check.

"I wanted to ask him about child support. It's maybe not exact, and I doubled it to help with the medical bills, but I felt it was only right."

Pink stained her cheeks. "I don't know what to say."

"Say you'll accept it. I know we're in a fucked up, weird as shit situation, and I want you to know I'm all in."

She looked at him sharply, body suddenly tense. "Did Bailey and Iris put you up to this? Because if so, no thank you." She held the check back out, mouth pulled tight. "Lulah and I were fine before we came to Prairie. We'll keep on being fine."

"Is that what you think this is?" he asked, anger flaring like a spark from the farrier's anvil. "That I'm trying to *buy you?*"

"Are you?"

He recognized the stubborn clench of her jaw. Lulah's was just like it when she got angry. It nearly made him laugh out loud. "Fuck, no. What's it going to take for you to believe that I'm in this for the long haul? How much longer are you going to judge me through a lens that's flat out wrong? Look—" he stood, vision hazing. "Take the money. Or don't. I'm trying to do the right thing. I want to be a part of your life. I want to be a father to Lulah, and I suppose I'm going to keep on trying. But for the love of all that is decent, stop judging me based on a false narrative."

With a cry of frustration, Suzannah stood, fisting the check. "You talk like you're the only one who was affected. Like you've been left out of the story—"

"I have."

"And I've been the one to endure it. To do everything I can to make sure our daughter is nurtured and provided for. I'm working just as hard as you are, and now you think a check is going to help me out when I have an emergency call on a Saturday afternoon at the clinic? You haven't offered to take her or babysit her *once*. Lulah needs a father, not a grown-up playdate."

That stung. "You won't let me be more than that. You're the one setting the rules of engagement."

"Yeah?"

"Yeah." He stood, too, breath coming in shallow gulps. "Fuck, Suzannah, I don't know how to get beyond this."

She shut her eyes, grimacing. "I don't either."

He pulled a hand through his hair. "I want to be with you and Lulah, but you have to meet me halfway."

She opened her eyes, wide, and blinked several times. "I'm afraid."

"Of what?" he asked softly.

Her cheeks flamed. "Of having my heart stomped on again," she whispered, looking down.

Her words sliced him to the quick. "Oh, sweetheart." He stepped into her space and pulled her against his chest, holding her tight. "I can't promise I won't be a dumbass, but I love Lulah. And I love you," he added, throat prickly. "I swear. If you let me, I'll be here every step of the way. We can figure out the tricky stuff."

Suzannah's shoulders shook. "I love you too. Lulah wants us to live together, I was all set to bring it up today, but then Iris and Bailey dogpiled on me, and got me worried that, that... I don't know. They were just worried, and that made me worried."

He placed his hands along the sides of her face and gently tilted up. "Look in my eyes."

She searched him, blue eyes pools of hope and fear.

"What does your heart tell you?"

"That you love us," she whispered.

"I do. With all my heart. And if you want to live

together, we can figure that out too. You know I want nothing more than that." He took a deep breath. He'd been thinking about this for weeks, and had finally approached his dad about hiring help. The conversation had been... less than pleasant, but in the end, Eddie had acquiesced. "I'd be willing to move into town."

She blinked.

She blinked again.

"I'll miss the ranch. I've never lived anywhere else except the college dorms, but I figure you need to be close to the clinic."

She nodded.

"So," he prodded, hardly able to breathe. "Are we doing this?" She had no idea she held his heart in the palm of her hand. A sudden move and he was toast.

A smile pulled her mouth wide. "Yes?"

"You've gotta say it with more conviction than that."

She nodded. "Yes," she said more firmly.

Gunnar's heart exploded from his chest, soaring on wings. A lightness came over him, ethereal, otherworldly. He dropped his head back, laughing. Then he swung her around, kissing her with all he had, not caring who saw. He had a family. And it might be complicated, it might not be perfect, but it was his and he loved his ladies with all his heart.

Chapter Twenty

*S*uzannah awoke to the soft sounds of Gunnar's alarm. Outside, a lone cardinal began his early morning serenade, even though in Suzannah's mind, it was still too dark to be early morning. Adjusting to Gunnar's sleep schedule had been...a challenge. Always more of a night owl, she preferred to view four a.m. as the end of a long night, not the beginning of a new day. Gunnar slapped the alarm and rolled over, pulling her into an embrace and slipping his hand between her thighs.

On the upside, she'd discovered four a.m. to be the perfect hour for uninterrupted trysts. Gunnar nuzzled her neck with a low growl, pressing his morning wood into her backside. "I was dreaming about you, just now."

"Mmm-hmm?" She rolled her hips, desire rapidly awakening all the cells in her body. "Is that why you're already hard?"

"Yep. You were spread out all gorgeous, and I had my face between your legs." As he spoke, he lightly stroked her pussy lips.

His words acted like a match to gasoline. Heat flooded her center.

He chuckled quietly, tongue flicking at the sensitive spot by her ear. "I love how it takes no time for you to be wet for me."

She squeezed the tops of her legs around his hand, looking for more friction. "I love your dirty mouth," she murmured back. They'd learned over the course of the last month that dirty talk was a sure-fire way to get them both off. There was something so illicit about whispering words like *fuck*, *pussy*, and *cock*, it took them from zero to light-speed in seconds. This morning was no different. Her breasts grew heavy, aching for his touch. Wiggling into him, she adjusted her position so she was cradled against him, one hand lazily stroking her pussy. She guided the other to her nipple, already tight, needing his touch.

Taking her cues, he gently rolled and pulled first one then the other. "Tell me how much you like that, babe." His breath set goosebumps rising across her chest.

"I love it. It makes my clit ache."

He groaned at her words, shifting to slide his cock between her folds. "You want me to touch that pretty little clit?" His fingers were everywhere, but where she wanted them.

Rolling her hips, she chased his fingers seeking more than the grazing, teasing strokes. "Yes, more." She pressed into him. A slightly different angle and he'd be there. Inside her, filling her, bringing sweet relief to the ache that continued to build in her core.

"Goddamn, baby," he rumbled, voice gravelly and thick. "I wanna fuck you bare so bad."

His words whipped her into a frenzy, clit pulsing, eager to be stroked until stars burst in her head. It was only with supreme effort she held back. "Can't," she panted. "Super sperm."

He nipped at her neck, voice hot in her ear. "Damn straight I have super sperm, and I wanna fill you up, baby." He circled her clit with a finger.

Need for him spiraled through her. Surely her IUD would be enough? Her Mirena IUD was over ninety-nine percent effective. Better than the condoms they'd used in Vegas. Could she trust it? Could she trust this next step between them? Yes, yes she could. And this time, if something happened, they'd face it together. Including the fear of another sick baby. She nodded, breathing deep. "Yes."

In a flash, he'd rolled onto his back, pulling her on top of him. His eyes were deep pools, she could drown in them. "What'd you say, baby?"

She canted her hips and reached between them, taking his cock and slowly guiding herself onto him. Every cell in her body sang with the joy of it, the feeling of homecoming, of connecting with him on such an elemental level. "I said yes. No more condoms." The look on his face burned into her soul. She'd remember this moment when she was old and frail. She moved, relishing the feel of him inside her, the heat, the friction, the intense throbbing building with each stroke. "I love you Gunnar."

He lifted his head, then, taking her mouth in a possessive kiss that left her dizzy, setting a rhythm with his tongue, with his cock that curled around her, invaded every pore, spiraled her higher and higher. His arms banded around her back, pulling her flush against him, so they touched everywhere, inside and out. She wanted this moment to spin out forever, her heart filled to bursting with love for him. He cracked her wide open, and the feeling was so big it couldn't be contained in her body. As they hurtled toward a climax, kissing, touching, rocking, tears leaked out of her eyes. Her mind went blank as her orgasm ripped through her, Gunnar followed and thrust hard – once, twice – their cries mingling as they continued to kiss, drinking every last bit of sensation from the cosmic explosion they'd shared.

Her bones melted. Suzannah couldn't move, didn't want to. If she moved, the magic moment they'd shared would be gone. She laid her head on his chest, taking comfort in the steady beat of his heart. His hand cupped her head. "Marry me, Suzannah. Let's make our family official?"

The tenderness in his voice, the cautious note of hope, acted like Cupid's arrow, and it hit its mark. She raised her head, searching his face. Nothing there but his heart on his sleeve.

"Once upon a time, you took a gamble. Would you do it again? Take a bet on us?"

If she spoke, she'd cry, so she nodded. "Yes," she whispered. "I will."

He kissed her again, tenderly, as if she was a precious treasure. "You and Lulah are my life," he rasped. "No matter what, I'll be there for you, and any other children my super sperm help create."

She shook with suppressed laughter, and then sighed, deeply satisfied. Too often, even now that he lived here, their coupling was hurried, not by choice, simply by necessity. Lying here with him, quietly talking in the aftermath, was a gift, however brief. "I wish we could spend the whole day in bed."

Gunnar squeezed her tight, covering her with kisses. "Mmmm, if only. I know what I'd do to you if we had the whole day." He grinned wickedly, giving her ass a little squeeze.

Neither of them would enjoy a luxury like that for some time, but it was nice to imagine.

"How about a shower instead?" He nuzzled the sensitive spot below her ear.

She rolled off him, and they snuck into the shower like two delinquent teenagers. Too soon, the water ran cold. They dressed quietly so as not to wake Lulah, and after a hurried cup of coffee, followed by more hurried kisses, they lingered on the porch.

"I can't stop smiling," Gunnar said, pulling her close.

She tilted her chin for more kisses. "I know, me either."

"We're really going to do it this time, right? No crossed wires, no waiting for hours wondering what's happened, just us becoming a family?"

"Sounds perfect to me."

Gunnar took her mouth, kissing her gently. "I don't want to leave you," he said when they parted.

"The sooner you go, the sooner you'll be home." She brushed her hands over his chest, delighting in the way his muscles filled her palms. "You'll be back for dinner?"

"With bells on and steaks for the grill. Should I bring a bottle of wine to celebrate?"

"Love it."

"Love you." Gunnar nuzzled her temple while squeezing her ass. He would never leave at this rate, not that she wanted him too.

"Don't you have horses to feed or something?"

"The guys can get started without me."

He'd hired a couple of Parker's firefighter buddies to help out part-time at the stables. She didn't know much about it, except that Gunnar seemed less stressed since he'd hired them and moved in, and that made her happy. She hated seeing his face drawn with worry. "Talk more tonight?"

"You bet, baby." He gave her one last lingering kiss, then tore himself away with a groan. "I'm going, I swear I'm going."

Suzannah covered her mouth, shaking with amusement as he walked backward to his truck, nearly tripping over Lulah's tricycle. "I'll be counting the minutes."

"I'll be counting the seconds."

"*GO,*" she giggled, shooing her hands at him. She stayed on the porch until his taillights disappeared, unable to stop smiling. This time, she was getting married for real. She couldn't wait to call Iris and Bailey.

Chapter Twenty-One

*S*uzannah returned to the house and headed for the kitchen, humming quietly under her breath. The stove clock glowed five-thirty a.m. Still plenty of time to tackle the endless paperwork before she needed to wake Lulah for school. She refilled her mug, grumbling. She might be blissed out, but even that didn't make her want to refrain from poking her eyeballs out over the hideous heaptons of paperwork the clinic generated. Worst was the billing. She never got the same answer twice from an insurance company, and she felt an obligation to fight for her patients. She had half a mind to hire a contract biller herself. Maybe even a medical transcriptionist. That would free up hours of her time. It was worth the out of pocket cost if she was able to spend more time with Lulah and Gunnar. She could catch up on sleep, too. What a novel idea.

But Gunnar would hate it. He'd insist she take it to the board, which she should, but already, she could detect a board fight brewing. When she'd given last month's report, the board had been evenly split over whether they thought she should continue doing everything, so for at least another month, she had to continue with the status quo. Suzannah swallowed her frustration. She was bound and determined to sail through the day with nothing but positive thoughts. She wasn't about to let a few grumpy people on the board ruin the first day of the rest of her life. With Gunnar. As a family.

No. Way.

Throwing back her coffee, she dug into the paperwork with newfound determination. She barreled through the stack at breakneck speed, staying focused on the pages until the phone startled her. Her stomach sank when she saw the caller id. "Hello?"

"It's Ivy."

Instantly, she was alert. "Are you okay? What is it?" She sounded like death warmed over.

"Something, I don't know what. Both Annie and I are out with fever and the works."

Both of them? Suzannah flew into doctor mode. "What are your symptoms?"

"One-hundred point one fever, vomiting and diarrhea both started after midnight."

Oh dear lord, the poor thing. "What about Annie?"

"Same," Ivy said hoarsely.

"Did you start having symptoms at the same time?" That could be the difference between a Salmonella outbreak and something like norovirus.

"Don't know."

"Do you have any idea what you ate yesterday?" That could offer a meager clue, but only if she remembered correctly.

"I have no idea. Maybe a fried egg on toast for breakfast, finishing off the friends' food for lunch, and leftovers for dinner."

She bit back a groan of frustration. If it was Salmonella, it could have come from anywhere, and she'd have to report it to the health department. In the meantime, what was she to do with Lulah? She was booked all day at the clinic. With the start of school, stragglers were clamoring for sports physicals. "Do me a favor and write it all down, if you can. And stick to clear liquids until you can keep something in your stomach. If you get worse, come into the clinic, and I can take a look. You'll probably be fine in a day or two."

As soon as she disconnected, she texted Gunnar.

S: *Babe, can you come get L? No school today — sick teachers! :(*

After a few minutes with no reply, she texted again.

S: *You there?*

Were there dead zones on the ranch? She shook off the macabre images of Gunnar lying in a gully, twisted and broken. He'd probably put down his phone. Irritating, but not that big of a deal. She still had an hour before the clinic opened. Deciding to let Lulah sleep a bit longer, she refilled her coffee and returned to her slowly dwindling stack of papers. But when thirty minutes had passed, a cool finger of deja-vu slithered down her spine.

No.

Absolutely not. This was *not* happening again. She slammed shut her laptop and reached for her phone, pushing her doubt back into the dark, fear-filled place where it lived. And where most days she could ignore it. She called this time. After six rings, it went to voicemail. Dammit, where in the hell was he? "Gunnar," she started, trying to keep the fear from her voice. "I need you to come get Lulah. School's canceled today and I've got to be in the clinic in thirty minutes. Call me? Please?" She began to pace the house, mind whirling. She didn't really have a backup. Martha and Eddie were in Oklahoma, and she didn't feel comfortable asking anyone else. Gloria McPherson was at reception today, and she supposed worst-case, Lulah could play behind the counter, but not all day. Maybe she could call Dylan's mom Addy? Yes. She'd call Addy. She scrolled through her contacts and dialed again.

Addy answered on the second ring.

"Addy, it's Suzannah. I'm in a bit of a bind this morning."

"Aren't we all?" she said wryly.

Guilt flushed her chest. But she could hear Iris admonishing her for not asking for help when she needed it. "I know, I'm sorry. I can't reach Gunnar, and I've got to open the clinic in less than an hour. Are you in a position to take Lulah for a little? Just until I can have Gunnar pick her up?"

"Sure. But I have to warn you, they're probably going to overdose on Baby Einstein today, since I work out of the house, and it looks like it's going to rain all day."

Suzannah cringed, but she understood. "One day won't hurt. I'll bring her over shortly."

Thirty minutes later, Addy answered the door, still in pajamas. "I hope it's okay we're still in jammies," she said with a smile.

"I envy you, although scrubs aren't too far from what you're wearing."

"That's why I like the medical field, comfy clothes for everyone."

Suzannah cocked her head. "What do you do?"

Addy lifted a shoulder and waved the children into the

living room. "Oh nothing glamorous at all, but it allows me to stay in Prairie and raise Dylan close to his grandparents. I do medical billing for a company in Kansas City. All remote."

Suzannah's jaw dropped. "How did I not know this about you?"

Addy shrugged. "I don't know. It's not that big of a deal, really."

Except that it was to her. "You and Dylan should come for dinner soon. We need to talk." If she could convince Gunnar of the need to hire someone like Addy, then maybe he could convince the stingier members of the board. Some of the board members, truly had no idea what it took to run a quality medical clinic. And why should they? They'd never had access to one. "'Bye, Lulah-bug," she called. "Daddy will be over to pick you up as soon as I can reach him."

"'Bye mama." She waved, already engrossed in playing blocks with Dylan.

"Thanks again, Addy."

Addy waved her off. "Happy to help. That's what neighbors are for."

When Suzannah arrived at the clinic, more than a little damp from the steady rain, half a dozen miserable looking people crowded the waiting room. What was going on? Gloria wasn't at her station, and after a quick scan, Suzannah spotted her in the corner, holding a trash can in front of Nita Cruz. "Gloria? What's going on?" She rushed over to where the women sat.

"Your regular appointment is here, as well as a walk-in with a possible broken finger. The others are all sick."

"How sick?" she said slowly, going over the symptoms Ms. Ivy had described.

Gloria motioned with her head toward Nita. "She

arrived, saying she'd been up half the night, and I managed to grab the trash can just in time."

Suzannah placed the back of her hand against Nita's forehead. Definitely fever. From the looks of it, Prairie was experiencing some kind of an outbreak. The question was, what kind? "Can you help Nita to the exam room? Let's take care of the acute patients first." She turned around and spoke to the room. "Good morning, everyone. Please bear with me, I'll see you all as soon as I can." Spinning on her heel, she followed Gloria and Nita back to the exam room. "Tell me what happened, Nita," she asked, walking directly to the sink and washing her hands.

"I woke up about two-thirty, feeling awful. Cramps, nausea, the works."

"And you're still having symptoms," Suzannah stated, confirming the obvious while she took Nita's temperature with a forehead scanner. One-oh-one. Enough to make a person feel like death warmed over. "Can you keep any liquids down?"

Nita shook her head.

"Well, it could be norovirus, but it could also be food poisoning." Suzannah pulled a clear plastic container from the cabinet. "Not very fun, but in order to properly diagnose food poisoning, I'll need to collect a stool sample."

Nita grimaced.

"Just be sure to thoroughly wash your hands, okay? And drink as many liquids as you can keep down. The biggest danger is dehydration."

Nita nodded, looking wretched.

"I'm sorry I can't do more."

All morning, her conversations mimicked the one she'd had with Nita. The clinic had never been so busy. Suzannah squeezed in her regular patients as she could, but by lunch, everyone in the waiting room was becoming testy. "Thank you all for your patience," she called as she pushed through the door from the back. "I don't want to shortchange anyone, and I promise, I will get to everyone."

"But I've been waiting an hour," someone called from across the room.

"I know, I know. It seems we're having an outbreak of some kind, and as soon as I can attend to you, I will. In the meantime, please make sure your paperwork is in order, that will help speed along the process." She glanced down at her clipboard and swallowed a groan. Mr. Appleberry, one of the most cantankerous board members, was next on the list. Just what she needed on a day when everything was flying out of control. Finding a smile, she searched the room. "Can I see Jonathan Appleberry?"

She glanced at her phone as she followed Jonathan and his wife into the exam room. Still no Gunnar. Fear gnawed at her. Lulah was safe, and she'd have to trust that Gunnar had somehow gotten her messages and knew where to pick up Lulah. She made a note to check with Gloria after the Appleberrys, maybe he'd left a message at the desk. Taking a deep breath and forcing a smile, she pushed into the exam room, and aimed for the sink. "How are you today Mr. Appleberry?"

"Not feelin' too chipper."

"That so?" She turned to study him. His color was off, and drops of sweat beaded along his hairline. Fever maybe? Onset of whatever bug had descended on the town?

"I feel kind of sick."

"Tell me more. Any nausea or vomiting?" She grabbed the blood pressure cuff from its place on the wall. "Let me take your vitals real fast." She wrapped the cuff around his meaty upper arm, and laid her stethoscope in the hollow of his elbow. She listened, alarm growing with each heartbeat. One-sixty-two over one-twelve. "Mr. Appleberry, your blood pressure is concerningly high. Do you take blood pressure medication?"

"Them pills the doc in Manhattan gave me in Manhattan about a year ago? Nah. He tried to tell me there was sumthin' wrong with my ticker. Ain't no one in my family ever had heart problems."

Great. A stubborn old man who probably had a heart condition.

"That you know of," interjected Mrs. Appleberry, face wrinkled in concern. "He was having trouble on our morning walk around the pond this morning. Kept having to stop."

"Oh?" This was not looking good. She suspected he needed to see a heart specialist immediately. "Are you experiencing any pain in your arm, or neck?"

Mrs. Appleberry's eyes widened. "He said he slept funny when he woke up."

"I see. Mr. Appleberry, I think you may be experiencing a heart attack. I'm going to have Gloria contact the heart clinic in Manhattan. I think you need to be seen by them immediately."

His jaw dropped. "What? That's over an hour and a half away."

"Which is why you should leave now."

"But you're the town doctor," he accused. "You're supposed to take care of us."

Suzannah bit her tongue and counted to five. This had been her number one frustration with the men and women who came to visit her. Prairie had been without medical care for so long, the residents assumed she could do it all. "Which I'm doing by referring you to a specialist, Mr. Appleberry. I'm a family practice doctor. I provide well checkups, I can give stitches if the injuries aren't too severe. I can set simple fractures. I'm not an emergency room, nor am I a specialist."

He frowned and opened his mouth to speak, but she held up her hand, putting as much command into her voice as she could. Just in the time that they'd been talking, his color grew more ashen. For the umpteenth time today, she wished that their facilities were more adequate. An hour-and-a-half drive could mean the difference between life and death. "Mr. Appleberry, if you refuse to go, I'm afraid something catastrophic could happen. In fact, I'm going to call over to the fire department and see if they can transport you by ambulance. I think you could benefit from some oxygen, and if you go into cardiac arrest on the drive, they will be able to attend you."

She pulled open the door and rushed to the front desk. Keeping her voice low, she spoke to Gloria. "I need you to call an ambulance for Mr. Appleberry, they need to take him to the heart clinic in Manhattan as fast as they can safely drive in that mess out there." She waved at the bank of windows. The rain was coming so hard it sounded like drums on the roof. Was Gunnar out in this mess? Was he okay? "And can you see if Dottie can check with Gunnar? I haven't heard from him, and I'm a little worried."

"Sure thing, sweetie pie – I mean doctor," Gloria corrected herself.

"Thanks." She hurried back to the Appleberrys. "Ambulance should be here in less than five minutes."

Mrs. Appleberry nodded, eyes round with worry. "Will he be okay?"

"That's my hope, Mrs. Appleberry. He'll be in good hands at the clinic."

In less than five minutes, a knock sounded at the door, and Parker stuck his head in. "Hey there Mr. A. I hear you're not feeling up to par."

"Darn tootin'," he grumbled.

"Well, we're gonna get you all sorted out, okay?" He eyed Suzannah. "Vitals?"

"B-p one-sixty-two over one-twelve, pulse ninety-six."

Parker's eyes flashed concern, but he was a pro, his face remained neutral. "Why don't you come with me Mr. A. Heart clinic knows we're on our way."

She mouthed a quick *thank you* to him over Mr. Appleberry's shoulder. "I'll follow up with you in a few days, all right?" She laid a hand on Mrs. Appleberry's shoulder and accompanied her to the front door. "Don't slip in the wet spots," she called. She peered up at the clouds. Gray as far as the eye could see. No chance of this letting up anytime soon. In fact, if it kept coming down this hard, they'd be contending with flash floods in a few more hours. Rolling her shoulders back, she marched to the receptionist's desk. She'd completed residency, she could manage a long day like today. Especially with Gunnar and Lulah waiting for her at the end of it. Before she grabbed the next clipboard from the top of the pile, she pulled her phone from her pocket one last time. Still nothing. She could feel the anxiety growing with each minute. This felt too much like Vegas. But it wasn't. They were in Prairie and Gunnar had just asked to marry her. There was a logical explanation for all of this. She fired off a quick text.

S: *everything ok? I'm worried :(*

With a sigh, she set her phone down on the counter and reached for the next clipboard. "Cash Aiken?" she called, pushing away the doubt and the worry that followed her like the rainclouds outside. She couldn't afford to think about her personal life until the waiting room had been cleared. No surprise, Cash displayed the same symptoms as everyone else, and as she was giving her spiel about staying hydrated, another knock sounded and Gloria peered in.

"I'm so sorry to bother, but Chief Castro is on the phone?"

"Don't tell me the fire department's sick, too?" She turned back to Cash. "You're free to go, now. Just remember to push liquids, and call if your symptoms worsen." She hurried down the hall to the phone. The waiting area seemed more crowded than before. What a nightmare. "This is Dr. Wilson."

Chief Castro got right to the point. "Doc. We need you. There's been a wreck about five miles west of town. Semi hydroplaned and crossed the line. Hit a school bus."

"Oh dear God."

"Marion's crew is coming, but they're twenty-five minutes away. Our ambulance is out—"

"Taking the Appleberrys," she breathed.

"And we need all the medics we can get. Estimates are maybe twenty on the bus."

"Ages?" Adrenaline surged into her body, even as her stomach sank. A head-on was bad enough, but on a bus with children and no seatbelts? This day could end in heartbreak for some families. "Doesn't matter, I'll be right there." She dropped the phone. And sprinted for the exit. "Emergency, Gloria. I need you to hold down the fort."

Chapter Twenty-Two

*E*arlier that day

When he'd arrived an hour late, Gunnar had been the recipient of a few knowing glances from Big Mike McAllister and Tony Cruz, Parker's firefighter buddies who moonlighted on various ranches around town. He'd been lucky to secure them when they were between jobs, and lucky for Hansen Stables, they were some of the best ranch hands around. They worked hard, but they made work fun. Gunnar had been working solo for so long, he'd forgotten how much he enjoyed the camaraderie of a shared day's work.

But he didn't mind their ribbing. Not today, when he was floating on air. He was marrying the love of his life, and soon the whole world would know about it. Even the sloppy weather couldn't get him down. The forecast had called for record-setting heavy rains over the next several days. He'd already discussed an action plan with the Sinclaires if Steele Creek, the creek that separated their two properties burst its banks. It had flooded just over a year ago during the tornado, but to date, the water had never risen high enough to take out the bridge. Even if the rains were record setting, the road into town should still be passable.

His phone buzzed. Why would Blake Sinclaire be calling again? They'd just talked not forty minutes ago. "'Sup?"

"Sorry to break it to you, but one of the young bulls got a little frisky with the fence line at the far end of the property."

"Are you fucking kidding me?" Today of all days.

"Well, it ain't April Fool's."

"Awesome. What do you suggest."

"It seems like a good chunk of the herd wandered in and decided to help themselves to your grass."

"What's a good chunk?"

"Forty head, maybe fifty?"

Goddammit. And those bison were wiley, too. It was going to take half a dozen people at least to round them up and push them into a gated pasture. And that would be all kinds of fun and games if it was raining. "What do you suggest?"

"Why don't you bring your guys out on your side? You'll spot 'em easy. Brodie, Ben, Hope and I will meet you there. As long as the creek doesn't get too high, we can push them over to our side. We have a fallow pasture that hasn't been grazed this season. We can hold 'em there until the fence gets repaired."

"Good deal. I'll see you in twenty, maybe thirty?"

"Sure thing."

Gunnar tucked the phone into his breast pocket. "Hope you brought your oilskins, boys. We gotta go take on a herd of bison." He *hated* rounding up bison. Cows, even longhorns, could be bossed, but no one bossed a bison. They could run as fast as a horse, and the last thing they wanted to do was start a stampede. If that happened, they could tear down the fences and run for miles. The Sinclaire herd was fairly docile, but they still didn't like being bossed. "Mike, why don't you grab Buzz, and Tony, you take Ricky. I'll saddle up Sugar. I think she's ready for something like this."

The men set to work, and in short order, they were headed towards the far end of the property at a clip, hats jammed low, oilskins buttoned tight to keep out the rain. Gunnar didn't need to remind them to the give the horses their heads in slippery conditions like this. They were expert horsemen, and their mounts were seasoned. Inside his coat, Gunnar felt the buzz of his phone. Whoever it was would have to wait, it was too wet and slippery to pull out his phone now. The last thing he needed today was a phone lost in the mud.

Sure enough, as the men crested the last rise on the far north edge of the Hansen land, he could see fifty, maybe sixty bison spread out. Squinting into the rain, he could see where the posts had been laid flat. The bison had marched on over and helped themselves to his prime grazing grass. "Damn fool beasts," he muttered under his breath. He understood the bottom line where bison were concerned, but when the damn animals got a bee in their bonnet, they wouldn't be contained. He waved, spotting his sister and the Sinclaire brothers further west. Gunnar's phone buzzed again. "Sorry, whoever you are." But what if it was Suzannah? If it was, it wasn't a social call. They might be in love, but they both were too busy for chit-chat calls. Indecision gnawed at him. She was probably okay. Hell, she was a doctor, if anything was going on with Lulah, she could handle it. More likely, it was probably a cold call from some company inviting them to lease farm equipment, or buy hay. He'd pretty much gotten to the point that he didn't answer the phone unless he recognized the caller. Sales calls wasted too much of his day.

"You could have picked a better day for this," Gunnar called out when they rode abreast.

Blake flashed him a grin. "You getting soft in your old age?"

"I'll never be as old as you," he volleyed back, good-naturedly. Blake had him by two years, but it didn't stop either of them from tossing around the old man jokes.

Brodie spoke up. "Ben thinks we oughtta swing wide to the east in a big horseshoe and slowly walk them back."

"Sounds good to me," Gunnar answered, sighing inwardly. Slowly walking the bison meant they'd move their horses forward a few yards and stop. Then they'd wait several minutes and do it again, all the time, not looking directly at the bison, keeping up a quiet conversation with each other in the hopes the bison would just ignore them, but move when they got too close. This would take until mid-afternoon, at least. "You know your livestock best."

"All right, then. Hope, why don't you and Gunnar come with me," Ben waved toward the east. "We'll be the farthest back. Some of you set a line here, so they don't drift farther south. We want to keep them in a bunch if possible."

The crew spread out to take their places. It was wet, boring work. By midday, even Gunnar's mood began to flag. They'd only just forded the creek, which was running high, but hadn't yet burst its banks. No doubt there would be flooding. The question was, how much? It was nearly two by the time Gunnar, Mike, and Tony rode into the barnyard, soaked. "Be sure to give the horses a thorough rub down. I don't want them getting chilled." He hung his oilskin on one hook, his Stetson on another, so they could dry, then he took care of Sugar, giving her an extra thorough rub down and currying. She'd been a champ, and the conditions had been miserable. Once she was settled, he pulled out his phone to see who'd called earlier. Great. It had died. He thought he'd charged it overnight, but maybe he hadn't. All he remembered was the feel of Suzannah curled up against him as she slept. He would never tire of it, the way she sighed deeply in sleep, the way he caught a hint of her perfume when he held her close.

"Why don't you call it a day, boys?" he called. Everything else on his list for the week would have to wait until the ground dried out. "Take a few days, and we'll see you after the rain stops?"

"Sounds good," Big Mike said. "I've got a new brew that's just about ready to tap. I'll bring some over."

Gunnar gave him the thumbs up, donned his oilskin and Stetson and made his way up the hill to the farmhouse. There were always chargers lying around in the main office. Leaving his wet clothes draped over the back porch rail and toeing off his boots, he entered the darkened farmhouse, stopping first in the kitchen to turn on the coffee machine. He could use a cuppa while he waited for his phone to charge. It was strange, being alone in the big empty house. It had been the heart of the ranch since before he was born. But more and more often, it stood empty while his parents traveled. He didn't begrudge them their adventures, they'd worked eight days a week his entire life. They deserved to slow down, to travel. And it pained him to think that one day the house, his home, would stand empty for other, sadder reasons. What then? Would strangers move in? The house had been occupied by Hansens for over one-hundred-fifty years. He could imagine Lulah tearing through the kitchen, or lounging on the bed in the room that had once been Hope's. Would

Suzannah entertain the idea once her contract had been fulfilled? So many possibilities, so much to talk about, but he was trying his best to go slow. To exercise the same patience in love as he did with horse training.

On the counter, his phone dinged to life, and a series of beeps in rapid succession signaled *someone*, or many some-ones had been trying to reach him. He reached for the phone, suddenly filled with apprehension, and scrolled through the long series of texts with growing distress.

S: *Babe, can you come get L? No school today – sick teachers! :(*

Shit. How long ago had she sent that? He glanced at the clock. Seven hours ago. Shit.

S: *You there?*

Oh this was bad. He'd let her down again. More texts followed.

S: *L is at Addy's. Please come get her when you can. Thx.*

Then one from Addy.

A: *Hey Gunn. Hope the rain isn't getting you down too bad. Lulah's over here with Dylan. Give me a ring when you're on your way. Or let me know if I need to bring her to you. :)*

And a final one from Suzannah.

S: *everything ok? I'm worried :(*

Motherfucker. He couldn't be in more hot water if he tried. Before checking the voicemail, he dialed Suzannah.

She wouldn't answer if she was with a patient, but at least she'd see he called. "Hey, darlin'. Everything's okay. Had to go chase down about sixty head of bison in the rain and my phone died. Just got back to the house. I'm on my way to get Lulahbelle right now. I just didn't want you to worry. I'll try and do a better job making sure my phone is charged. Love you."

Next, a quick call to Addy to let her know he was on his way. "Addy?" he asked when she answered.

"Everything okay? I was starting to worry."

He raked a hand through his hair. "Everything's fine except we had to go push a load of bison outta one of our fields. Took most of the day. I'm on my way in for Lulah."

"Sure, no problem. She's lying on the couch right now. I think she and Dylan wore each other out."

"Thanks again, Addy. See you soon." He pulled the charger from the wall, stuffing it in his pocket along with the phone. He'd charge it in his truck as he drove. Overhead, the metal roof sounded like a stampede as a particularly heavy band of rain passed through. He hurried out to the truck and headed into town. As he crossed the bridge where Steele Creek passed underneath the road, he glanced over. The stream was an angry, brown, roiling snake. If the heavy rain didn't let up, it wouldn't take long to overrun the road. He pushed his speed heading into town, and for a moment, thought about bringing Lulah home to the bungalow. But if the road washed out, there'd be no one to take care of the animals. No, he'd have to stay out at the farm, just in case. But maybe he could bring Suzannah out if the water didn't rise any further. He smiled at the thought of the three of them playing house together out at the ranch. Maybe that would be just the thing to convince Suzannah to live out there someday.

Addy's front door was open when he pulled up. He

dodged the puddles on the walkway and rapped on the screen door. "Door's open, come on in," Addy called.

He stepped gingerly inside, aware that his oilskin was soaked through. He called quietly over to where Lulah lay on the couch. From where he stood, she looked plum tuckered out. "Hey there Lulahbelle. You ready to go?"

She nodded, not moving.

"You okay, baby girl?"

She nodded again, but she didn't look okay. Maybe she was just tired. Hadn't Suzannah mentioned that the children took naps every day at preschool? Wiping his feet on the mat, he crossed to the couch and squatted down. "Time to go. Can you get up?"

"Can you carry me?" she whined.

Man, she must really be tired if she was whining.

"Sure thing, but let's put on your raincoat. I'm pretty wet."

She slid off the couch, moving with the speed of a snail. Gunnar refrained from tapping his foot. The urge to get back to the ranch was becoming stronger with each gust of wind and heavy rain. "Can I help you, honey?"

"No." She pouted. "I can do it myself."

"Okay, but let's get a move on. Once we're home, I can take you down to check on Batman." Usually, the opportunity to go visit her horsey was all the encouragement she needed. Not so today. The rain must be getting her down. After what felt like a small ice-age, she held up her arms, ready to be picked up. "Come on, let's go, baby girl. Thanks again, Addy," he called.

"You bet," she hollered from her office. "Catch you 'round. Suzannah said something about dinner soon."

"Sounds good to me. See you, Dylan." He raised his hand to Addy's son, who waved then promptly returned to his lego project.

Gunnar raced to the truck and yanked open the door, pulling the seat forward and setting Lulah down in the car seat. As soon as she was settled, he jogged around to the other side and started the truck. The rain came down so heavy in spots, it was hard to see the road. Not that it bothered him, he knew the roads around Prairie like the back of his hand, but some of the dips and turns could be treacherous in gullywashers like today.

He slowed as he hit Steele Creek, a prickle of concern slithering down his neck. The water was maybe a foot below the road. At least his parents had a deep freeze. If he and Lulah had to hole up for a few days, they'd be well stocked. Maybe it would even be fun. A little extra father-daughter time. Gunnar checked the rear-view. Lulah had been awfully quiet the entire drive. Sure enough, she was sacked out. He'd do his best not to wake her. But when he got her inside and into a kitchen chair, her cheeks were flushed. And when he unbuttoned her raincoat and removed it, her chest felt warm. He had no idea where to look for a thermometer, but he'd bet his favorite pair of boots his baby girl had a fever. Suzannah would know what to do, but again, she didn't answer his call. "Hey, babe. I've got Lulah, and we're back at the ranch, but I think she's got a fever. Can you give me a call and tell me what to do? Also, what do you think about coming out here tonight? The river looks ready to overrun the road, and I'm gonna need to keep an eye on the livestock. I'd sure love your company."

Fear settled in the pit of his stomach. She was okay, wasn't she? This wasn't some kind of weird revisiting of Vegas, was it? He pushed the thought away. There was no way Suzannah would abandon them. Not a chance. She must be slammed at the clinic. He'd see her soon enough. "Daddy?" Lulah's eyes flickered open, and her face was all screwed up. Come to think of it, she looked a bit green around the gills.

"What is it, sweetheart? You feelin' okay?"

"Daddy?" her voice held a note of panic, and her eyes grew wide.

In slow motion, it dawned on him what was happening, but before he could grab a bowl or jump out of the way, her stomach made a sickening gurgle, and his sweet little angel emptied the contents of her stomach all over the floor. And him.

Chapter Twenty-Three

*O*hshitdamnmotherfuckerwhatthefuckamIsupposedtodonow?

Lulah let out a keening wail of horror. "I want mommy," she bawled.

"I know baby girl, I want mommy too."

Towel. He needed a towel. Breathing through his mouth, he opened the cabinets searching for the towels. Jesus. He'd lived here most of his life, why couldn't he find the towels. Who went and rearranged shit after he'd moved out? He found them in a bin underneath the sink. "It's gonna be okay, sweetie pie, just let me—"

Her stomach made that awful sound again, and somehow, with the speed of one of the Crouching Tiger characters, he managed to whip out the trash can and catch most of the contents as they hurtled out of her. Oh, his poor girl.

Now she was sobbing loudly, screaming for Suzannah.

"I know, I know, honey." He could hardly think through the buzzing in his ears. "Let's get you cleaned up. Here." He wiped off her face and threw another towel on her lap. He grabbed a third towel and tossed it to the floor.

He'd get the sick cleaned up later, but right now he had to get her out of her clothes. Wait. Water. She needed water. Her mouth must taste like shit.

He filled a glass and handed it to her. "Take a sip and spit it out, okay? It will make your mouth taste better." He held out the trash can. Thank heavens she was old enough to know how to spit out water. He set the glass on the table. "Okay, let's get you out of these clothes." He helped her pull her arms inside her shirt. Fuck, she definitely had a fever, her torso felt like a furnace.

"C-c-cold, Daddy," she chattered when he'd tossed her shirt to the floor.

"I know sweetie. You don't feel good. But we're gonna get you all better. Let's get you out of these yucky pants."

Gunnar worked as fast as he could, pulling off shoes then socks, stripping her down to the Spiderman underpants she insisted on wearing. Picking her up, he carried her upstairs to his parents' room. "Let's see if we can find one of Besta's shirts to put on." He rifled through her drawers until he found a K-State tee. It would be enormous on Lulah, but it was clean. He pulled it over her head. "Here you are, baby. Now you're a Wildcat."

"I want mommy." Her lower lip stuck out, trembling.

"I'm gonna call her right now. Here, why don't you crawl under the covers? I'll be right here." He pulled back the bedspread and helped her settle. Keeping his hand on her back, doing his best to soothe his sweet girl, he dialed Suzannah again. "Hey there. So, ah… we had a little incident…"

"I'm sick mommy," Lulah wailed.

Great. That was sure to worry Suzannah unnecessarily. "But I've got it under control." At least as much as he could right now. "So, ah… give us a call?"

He puffed his cheeks, blowing out a breath. What in

the hell was he supposed to do? He hadn't read the *What to do when your baby gets sick* chapters in the parenting books, because he figured Suzannah would always be around to take care of Lulah if she got sick. And of course, his books were stacked on the bedside table in the bunkhouse. To make matters worse, his laptop was back at the bungalow. But his phone. He could google from his phone. He punched in '4yo fever vomiting'. He scanned the results, growing more terrified with each entry. Meningitis? Measles? Scarlet Fever? It seemed fever and vomiting could be attributed to everything from mild childhood illness to life-threatening situations. And how was one supposed to know the difference? He closed the browser and scrolled through his contacts. Maddie would know, and she researched everything.

"Hey, Gunn. Blake mentioned you had quite a morning."

He cut right to the chase. "Lulah just puked all over the kitchen floor, and she's burning up. I have no idea where the thermometer is, or what to do, and I can't reach Suzannah." Fuck. He sounded pathetic. He tried to keep the concern from his voice, but this shit was serious. How was he supposed to help his baby girl? Worse, what if this somehow damaged her heart? He froze, stomach hollow, hands trembling.

Maddie muffled the phone, and he could hear a deep voice responding to whatever it was that she'd said. "Hang tight. I'll be over in a few."

"I'm upstairs in mom and dad's bedroom. Back door is open."

Twenty minutes later, Maddie still hadn't arrived. Gunnar paced the bedroom floor as Lulah slept fitfully. Is this what it had been like for Suzannah when she'd found out about Lulah's heart? Had she experienced the same sense of sick helplessness, the paralyzing fear? No. It had to have been a thousand times worse for her. Still, he was more than a little freaked out. What if this was something more serious than the flu? She was his world, and he couldn't imagine her not in it.

He picked up the phone to try Suzannah again, just as Maddie's name appeared on the screen. "Where are you?" he barked.

"Road washed out. I'm so sorry."

He fisted his hand, swallowing a curse. And took a deep breath. "What do I do? Tell me what to do?"

"I think your mom has some children's Motrin in her medicine cabinet. I brought it over when Henry was teething."

"Is it still good?" He was already at the top of the stairs, bounding down two at a time. If his mother hadn't 'rearranged' it, the cupboard closest to the back door held first aid supplies.

"It should be fine."

He flung open the cabinet, rifling through the bottles until he found a purple and white bottle marked *Children's Motrin*. "Found it."

"And you're sure it's marked for children?"

"Yep. And it's got one of those cup things."

"Okay, good. She's probably just got a little bug, Gunn. It's nothing to worry about. I promise."

Tell that to the fear monster currently chewing through his belly. "What if—"

"Gunnar," Maddie cut in firmly. "Chill. She's fine. Kids get sick all the time. You can handle this. A colicky horse is much more serious."

Oh.

Well, yeah. That was a life-threatening situation for the horse. "So are you saying I'm overreacting?"

Maddie chuckled. "Just a little. But it's understandable. The first time Henry got a fever, I called your mom, terrified. Just be sure to make her drink plenty of fluids, even if she doesn't like it. Little kids get dehydrated super quick."

Fluids. He could do fluids like a champ. "I'll call if I need anything else." He hung up and grabbed the water glass he'd left on the table and took it upstairs with the medicine. He measured out the grape flavored goo, and then gently shook Lulah. "Here princess, this will make you feel better."

She made a face and shook her head back and forth. "Yucky."

"I know, but we've gotta get your fever down."

"Where's mommy?"

The question punched him in the gut. He wanted her just as badly. "She's stuck at work hon. But she'll get here as quick as she can." He had no idea how that would work with the road washed out, but he'd tell her anything to get her to take her medicine. "Please, honey? Let's just take a sip." He airplaned the purple goo. "On three. One, two, three." Surprisingly, it worked, and she opened her mouth, then promptly grimaced. "Good girl. I'm so proud of you." Lulah glared at him, and if hadn't been so worried, he'd have laughed. He drew his finger down her nose. "I love you, baby girl. I'm always gonna be right here for you, 'kay?"

"Love you too, Daddy," she murmured, eyes growing heavy.

Gunnar's throat squeezed tight. His heart thumped harder, feeling like it might burst from his ribs. Until this moment, he'd never experienced anything more beautiful in the world than a sunrise in the Flint Hills. But hearing the words *I love you* from the mouth of his child, his sweet angel, sick as she might be, eclipsed everything. He'd had no idea his heart could become so full, and yet here it was, painfully expanding right out of his chest. He dropped a kiss onto her hot forehead, squeezing his eyes shut and committing the moment to memory. This moment would be one he remembered on his deathbed.

Rising, he went to the window and pulled back the curtain. The rain still came down, but not so heavy at the moment. He grabbed the phone and sent a text to Suzannah, wanting to outline half a dozen concerns, at least. Instead, he settled for keeping it simple.

G: *Gave Lulah Motrin. And water.*

With another curse, he tossed the phone to the far side of the bed, trying his damndest not to give in to irritation over not reaching her. This was his karmic payback for not answering the phone earlier. Served him right for ignoring her when she needed him. He'd feel better once he heard Suzannah's voice, and received her assurance that Lulah was fine. But he handled thousand pound beasts for a living, a toddler's illness wasn't about to bring him to his knees.

Careful to avoid waking Lulah, he settled himself next to her, placing a hand on her back, to reassure himself she was still breathing. There was nothing to do now, but wait. He shut his eyes and tried to calm his breathing. Suzannah would call as soon as she got off work.

It was dark when the phone startled him from a dreamless sleep. "Suzannah?" he mumbled, groggy.

"Gunnar it's Dottie. I'm at the hospital with Suzannah."

Chapter Twenty-Four

*G*unnar sat bolt upright, adrenaline turning his mouth to copper. "*WHAT?*" Next to him, Lulah started. He lowered his voice. "Where is she? Is she okay? *What happened?*" He clutched the bedspread, willing her with all his heart to be okay. He couldn't lose her, not after all they'd been through, not after what they'd shared this morning. It didn't matter that this morning felt like years ago. He glanced over at Lulah, sleeping peacefully now that the medicine had kicked in, hardly able to breathe. His family would not be snatched from him like this.

"She's got whatever this bug that's going around and got very dehydrated. Passed out when she returned to the clinic. Fortunately, Gloria was still there and heard the crash."

"Wait. Where had she been?" Gunnar offered a silent word of thanks to Gloria, picturing what might have happened if Suzannah had been alone.

"I don't have all the details. Some big accident west of town. She went to help."

"Of course she did." Because she never said no when it came to taking care of others. He scowled, grim determination settling in his bones. That was it. As soon as she was well, they were going to have a chat about her self-care, or lack of it. He'd brought it up a few times over the month they'd lived together, once he'd realized how she was burning the midnight oil on paperwork. But the second he raised the issue, she firmly shut him down. No more. Not when she was jeopardizing her safety. "Where are you?"

Via Christi. But don't you dare think of dragging that sick little girl up here. Suzannah's gonna be fine. She's sleeping right now and they want to keep her overnight for observation. She hit her head when she collapsed, but they don't think she has a concussion. Just a goose-egg."

"You sure she's gonna be okay?"

"I promise. I'm gonna spend the night up here with a friend of mine, and I'll bring her right to you as soon as they release her. Don't you worry about a thing, except keeping Lulah full of fluids."

"Noted." He snuck a peek at her, then looked at her water glass, still mostly full. As soon as he got off the phone, he'd wake her up and make her take a drink.

"We need to talk about the clinic."

"We need to close the clinic until further notice," he growled. "I don't want it reopened until we have a board meeting and we agree to hire some additional help. We were naive to think one doctor would be enough."

"I don't disagree. You know that. But you also know who's going to have a conniption."

"I don't give a rat's ass if Sanchez, the Brewer, or the Appleberrys quit the board over this. We burned her out and I won't stand for it."

"Glad to see you finally stepping into the role," Dottie answered wryly. "I'll make calls once—"

Gunnar cut her off. "No. *I'll* make the calls, and I'm gonna make it damn clear I won't tolerate any shenanigans when we meet."

～

"Drink your water, baby doll." Gunnar held out the plastic cup toward Lulah as they sat on the back porch slider.

She took the cup with her pudgy hands and pretended to sip.

"More," Gunnar said. "Did you even take a sip?"

Lulah giggled and shot him a sly grin.

The tight knot that had taken up residence in his chest over the last few days began to loosen. Her laughter delighted him, and assured him she'd come through her bout of norovirus with flying colors.

"When will mommy be here?"

"Two winks."

She blinked her eyes. "One… Two. Is she here yet?"

He reached over to tickle her. "No, silly girl. I bet she'll be here in fifty seconds. Can you count to fifty?"

He couldn't blame Lulah's impatience. He was as antsy to see Suzannah as she was. He'd had the scare of his life with both of them, and he just wanted to touch her, hold her, assure himself she was still flesh and bone.

Lulah counted to fifty three times before he heard Dottie's car on the long drive. "She's here, princess."

Lulah bounced on the seat next to him. He bounced with her, triggering peals of laughter. "You're not 'posed to do that, daddy."

"No? Why not? I'm excited to see mommy too." He

bounced some more, just so he could hear her laugh another time. And to hide his nervous anticipation. When she stepped out of Dottie's car, he jumped off the slider, grinning like a damned fool. But ask him if he cared? His heart just kept expanding the deeper he fell for the ladies he loved.

He stopped within touching distance, drinking her in. It had only been a little over forty-eight hours since he'd left her standing on the porch, lips plump from their kissing, yet it felt like a lifetime.

Lulah launched herself at Suzannah with a shout. "*Mommy!*"

Suzannah swept Lulah into her arms. "I heard you were sick."

Lulah nodded. "But Daddy tooked care of me."

Suzannah slid a glance his direction. "Did he, now?"

"He let me have popsicles."

"*Did he, now?*"

Busted. But Lulah liked them better than water, and since they were stuck in the house...

"Totally okay," she said in his direction. "I'm just glad to be home."

He couldn't stop smiling. "Hi, beautiful," he said when she turned his direction, Lulah on her hip.

Her smile matched his, lighting her face like sunshine. "Hi. I missed you."

He pulled both his ladies close, inhaling deeply as Suzannah ducked under his chin. "I was so worried."

"Me too." Her arm wrapped around him, squeezing tight for emphasis.

"Don't ever let me go."

"Never. You either."

"No way. You're stuck with me."

She tilted her chin, eyes shining. "Promise?

"Yes. You?"

She nodded, smile widening, letting out a small laugh when Lulah interjected. "Is this a Lulah sandwich?"

Dottie joined in their laughter, and Gunnar could have sworn her eyes were a little misty. "See you at the diner at seven?"

Gunnar nodded, growing serious again. "Hope and Ben offered to take Lulah during the meeting.

"Suzannah," Dottie said briskly. "Don't you worry about a thing. Understand?"

Suzannah checked the notes on her tablet one last time as Gunnar pulled into the mud-filled parking lot next to Dottie's Diner. A typically fifteen-minute drive had expanded into a forty-five-minute adventure thanks to Steele Creek still running over the bridge next to the Hansen spread. But Lulah was happily ensconced at home with Auntie Hope and Uncle Ben, whose drive had been much shorter. She shook off the trepidation that lurked at the edges of her conscious. She'd created an airtight proposal. If the board didn't go for it, well… she had some serious thinking to do if they didn't.

Gunnar reached across the dash and gave her arm a squeeze. "You've got this, babe. We've got this. Your ideas are fantastic. Prairie could become a model for rural communities across the west."

"Do you think they'll go for it?"

"They're fools if they don't." His hand moved to the base of her skull. "Are you okay with a kiss?"

Butterflies took flight in her belly. "I've been fever free for over twenty-four hours. You?"

"No fever. I feel great." His mouth drew up into a sly smile. "And I'll feel a helluva lot better when you let me kiss you."

She bit her lip, but even that wasn't enough to stop the goofy grin from spreading across her face. "They say laughter is the best medicine," she started, a breathless note to her voice. "But really, it's kissing."

Gunnar's eyebrows shot up, eyes crinkling with mirth. "That so?"

She nodded. "My expert medical opinion."

Desire flickered in his eyes. "Well, I'm not one to disobey doctor's orders."

She met him halfway, jamming her fingers into his hair, kissing him like she'd been starved. He kissed her back until she was dizzy, breath coming in shallow bursts. She'd have happily stayed in the truck, necking, but a rap sounded at Gunnar's window.

"You're fogging up the windows, kids." Blake Sinclaire admonished with a smirk. "You might want to refrain until after the board meeting? Don't want to give anyone reason to accuse you of conflict of interest." He winked and took Maddie by the hand, helping her navigate the parking lot-turned-moat.

"I know a great place we can go park after this meeting is over," Gunnar suggested, half-serious.

"I still have keys to the clinic," she countered with a with an innocent pout.

Gunnar let out a low chuckle that made her belly jump with anticipation. "That's what I love about you, 'Zannah. You always go for the naughtiest option."

"Only with you."

"Banter aside." He turned serious. "Are you ready?"

Her mouth drew down as she nodded. Joking aside, the stakes were high tonight, and they both knew it.

He offered his knuckles for a fist bump. "Well let's go kick ass. Stay there." He hopped out and jogged around the front of the truck, opening the door and extending his hand.

These little gestures melted her, and built her confidence. With Gunnar by her side, she could do anything. Holding fast to his hand, they walked into the diner, and even when a dozen pairs of eyes turned her way, she didn't falter. Not in the least. She drew herself up to her full height and entered the diner like it was her realm. "Good evening, everyone."

Gunnar gave her hand a final squeeze before he let go and moved to take his place at the head of the tables pushed together. She took a seat a few tables away, reviewing her notes but keeping half an ear on the proceedings. Present were Dottie, Blake and Maddie, Gloria McPherson, Nita Cruz and her son, Tony. Those were the votes she could count on. On the other side of the table sat the ones that needed convincing. Jonathan and Bobbie Appleberry, Judge Brewer, Diana Sanchez, and Chief Cruz and his wife, Amelia.

She'd treated or worked with every person on the board, and as Gunnar brought the meeting to order, she fervently hoped her proposal would be compelling enough. The first half of the meeting was business as usual – the reading of minutes, the presentation of the budget by Judge Brewer, their treasurer, motions and amendments related to an upcoming fundraiser. Silence fell on the group. Gunnar motioned for her to join the table. Her stomach dropped like she was in the last car of a roller-coaster. Gathering her nerve, she stood and crossed to the open seat at the table, on Gunnar's right. She could do this.

Gunnar began. "As you're all well aware. Prairie experienced a recent outbreak of norovirus that pretty much brought us to our knees. No one went unscathed, including Dr. Winslow."

She was grateful he'd left Lulah out of it. Their only path forward lay through professionalism, not playing up their relationship.

"In the lead-up to that incident, you will remember that the board has had many… ah, healthy discussions on whether or not we've asked too much of Dr. Winslow."

Suzannah watched the board members for any clue of where they might be on the issue. It was like watching a tournament of high-rolling poker players in Vegas. Everyone around the table sat stony-faced, not giving away a thing.

Gunnar continued. "Regardless of where we were on that day before the outbreak, I think we can all agree that Dr. Winslow was unequivocally overwhelmed on that day, and unable to perform her duties as we had envisioned."

The sick feeling returned to Suzannah's stomach as heads began to nod. Dear God in heaven, they were going to sack her and then the collectors would come after the Hansen property. She couldn't let that happen. No matter what. She'd take four jobs if necessary, wash dishes at Dottie's. She wasn't above that, she had a family to protect.

Gunnar's voice hardened. "That day, it became patently obvious that we'd asked way too much of Dr. Winslow. We looked for and hired a family practice doctor. What we needed that day was a fully operational critical care clinic. I think we can all agree, those are two very different job descriptions?" He paused long enough to look each board member in the eye and secure a nod before continuing. "Good. I'm glad to see we're all on the same page. Jonathan—" he turned to Mr. Appleberry. "I understand you were in the clinic that day, yes?"

He nodded, mouth formed into a perfect cartoon-like frown.

"And you would have benefitted from critical care, yes?"

Mr. Appleberry nodded again, frown deepening.

"And, I understand from Parker Hansen you coded on the ambulance ride to Manhattan?"

"Dr. Winslow saved his life," Mrs. Appleberry interjected, giving her husband a formidable glare. "Jonathan was upset, and worried about the cost, but he'd have died if Dr. Winslow hadn't insisted he be transported to the heart clinic.

She could hug Mrs. Appleberry right now.

"Exactly." Gunnar swung his arm as an exclamation point. Suzannah bit her cheek to keep from grinning as pride filled her. If he ever gave up horses, he could be a lawyer in a hot second. "Which brings me to my proposal, prepared with the help of Dr. Winslow. Prairie... *this region* desperately needs a hospital. At the very least, a critical care center. We've been outfitted with equipment we don't have the capacity to use, and if we built out, hired more doctors, technicians, and administrators, not only could we bring much-needed jobs to the region, but we could serve the wider community. How many Jonathan Appleberrys haven't made it to the heart clinic in time? Catastrophic accidents with equipment are the leading cause of death in the farming and ranching community. How many could we save if we expanded our offerings? If the tornado had happened today, my uncle Warren, Maddie's dad—" he gestured to her. "*Still* wouldn't have survived. Why? Because we hired a family practice doctor, not an emergency room team of surgeons, anesthesiologists, x-ray techs, nurses and therapists. I hate admitting that, but gang, that's the truth." He looked at each person again before continuing. "And I think we all realize that. But before I entertain a motion to expand our clinic into a regional hospital or critical care clinic, I want you to hear from the expert in the room." He swung the weight of his gaze to her, and it lit her up from the inside. Whatever happened next, Gunnar was all in for her.

She stood, rolling her shoulders and stepping forward. "Thank you, all. I'd like to start with this simple graph…"

Bit by bit, question by question, she drew them in, defending her numbers and her sources, sharing anecdotes from her time both at Research Medical Center and the Kansas City Free Clinic. Her throat began to dry, someone, Dottie, maybe, place a glass of water in her hand. After two hours, she faltered. "I-I'm sorry. I have to sit." She wasn't sure what else she could say. She felt like the Appleberrys were with her, and Chief Castro. But his wife wasn't, and neither was Judge Brewer.

Gunnar stared down the board, grim determination on his face. "I believe we have a majority, but I'd feel better if we moved forward with a unanimous vote. Prairie needs this. Our neighboring communities need us to take the lead on this. But I think I know what's holding a few of you back. And that's my relationship with Dr. Winslow."

Suzannah flashed hot from head to toe. All eyes turned to her, and she was sure she was as red as the cherries in Dottie's cherry pie. Maybe it would be better if the earth opened up and swallowed her whole. She stared at Gunnar, trying to tell him with her eyes that whatever he had planned, it was a bad idea. He was her strongest advocate on the board. They'd sack her for sure if he stepped down, and her spidey sense was going crazy. He was going to step down. She shook her head imperceptibly. But he wasn't looking at her, dammit. And she was sure that was intentional.

Gunnar looked straight at Judge Brewer. "I think there are some of you who feel I have a conflict of interest."

"Well you *are* shacking up with her," Mr. Appleberry grumbled.

Gunnar's eyes turned to ice. "Yes. I am. And we share a beautiful daughter together, the most amazing gift in the world. And I intend to marry Dr. Winslow as soon as she'll let me. So, yes. We're 'shacking' up together." He air quoted. "Which is why I'm going to ask the board to accept my resignation, effective immediately."

Mrs. Sanchez gasped. Maddie's hand flew to her mouth, eyes wide. Dottie turned purple. "Don't you *dare* do a damned fool thing like that, Gunnar Hansen. I swear I will go find Warren and bring him back to personally tan your hide."

He flashed her a grin as he shook his head. "I appreciate the sentiment, Dottie. You know I do. But this is for the best. And if it will convince Judge Brewer, and Mrs. Castro and Mrs. Sanchez, that we need a hospital, then it's absolutely the right thing to do, and Warren would expect nothing less from a Hansen." He turned to Maddie, eyes softening. "I'm sorry, Maddie Jane. I know you wanted one of us to lead the board, but your vision is best served by someone more objective than me."

Maddie looked like she was ready to cry. Suzannah wanted to join her. She wasn't prepared for this. Warren's legacy meant everything to the Hansens.

Gunnar turned to her and took her hand. "I'm crazy in love with this woman. I can't think straight when I'm around her, and I only want what's best for her, and our daughter."

"And Prairie," Suzannah added, voice tight.

He nodded once. "And Prairie. But that means I shouldn't be president of the board." He laced his fingers through hers and turned back to the table. "But I do have a person in mind who will be an outstanding board president. I've already talked to him, and he's willing. He has hospital board experience, access to deep pockets for fundraising, and is committed to staying in Prairie. I nominate Jason Case to by my replacement."

"But he's not even here," Chief Castro sputtered.

"Nope. Have him in for an interview. Some of you know him already, and I think you'll agree with me that he's the real deal, and can take our clinic to the next level. For those of you who haven't met him? Prepare to have your minds blown." Gunnar pulled her arm around his waist, fingers still locked with hers, and turned to her, eyes bright. "But as of tonight, I'm officially a family man and Dr. Winslow's biggest fan."

Chapter Twenty-Five

ctober 28ᵗʰ

Gunnar paced in the kitchen of the farmhouse, the sounds of the bonfire drifting in through the screen door. The night was perfect. Crisp and cool, not muggy, and no bite to the air. His sister, Hope, wearing devil horns and looking ready to pop with the newest addition to the Hansen-Sinclaire clan, entered the kitchen from the upstairs. "Are you ready?" She beamed. "They look gorgeous."

Gunnar shook out his hands. "More than ready. I've been on pins and needles all afternoon."

Hope pulled him into a hug. "Aww, my big bwave bwover is nervous."

"Stop with the baby talk," he grumbled.

"No way," she laughed. "Payback, big brother." They shared a look that said so much. Hope blinked rapidly. "Seriously. Ben and I couldn't be happier. Even if I didn't get to pull all the revenge pranks I've been planning for years."

"I'll always be two steps ahead of you, Hopey," he teased, reverting back to a name he used to torture her with when they were younger.

She gave him a wicked grin. "Maybe, maybe not. Just remember who's wearing the horns." She winked and waddled outside.

He had to give his kid sister credit. The costume party and bonfire had been her idea. He and Suzannah had wanted something low-key, but that still involved their friends. And they hadn't wanted to wait until Thanksgiving or Christmas. The kicker? Since everyone was in costume, none of their guests suspected a thing. No one questioned his Old West get-up. To be honest, it wasn't far off from his dress duds, but he thought he resembled a rather dapper version of Wild Bill Hickok, wearing a trim velvet coat and a ribbon tie.

He turned at the sound of heels on the stairs. Suzannah's friends, Iris and Bailey, appeared, all smiles. Winning them over had been hardest of all, but in the end, the sweetest victory. And he loved them for loving Suzannah with a sisterly fierceness that came from a friendship forged in fire. Iris spoke first. "Have the ring?"

"And the necklace."

"Good man," said Bailey.

Iris pulled him into a hug and kissed his cheek. High praise. "You're a good man, Gunnar."

"Especially with us to keep you on the straight and narrow," teased Bailey.

"I'll have the last laugh when you fall hard and fast and get married inside of a week," he predicted.

"Bring it, cowboy, bring it."

"Is she ready?" he asked, ready to run upstairs and carry her down himself. Judge Brewer was waiting on the porch, into his third cup of witch's brew. If they waited much longer, he'd be in his cups, and come hell or high water, he was marrying his woman tonight.

"Patience, grasshopper. You can't rush perfection."

"Speaking of," Bailey cocked her head to the stairs, where his perfect little angel stood shyly, clutching a bouquet of roses covered in glitter."

He dropped to his knees. "Look at you." Heaven help him when she became old enough for prom. He'd be a puddle. "Come here, princess. You're beautiful." Lulah had been very excited about the costume party, but had insisted on being a Batman princess, and she refused any help with her costume. She wore the pink sparkly dress he'd given her the first day he'd met her, with her pink and black Batman cape Iris had made, and a crown of black and silver bats. His girl, original to the core. "Are you ready?"

She nodded, all smiles.

He could not possibly love her more than he did right now. "Is mama ready?"

"She's bootiful." Lulah turned as Iris and Bailey parted like the Red Sea, and there, standing on the bottom step stood his beautiful bride.

He was gonna need a pacemaker, because his lungs just gave out and his heart froze. Emmaline Andersson had outdone herself. She'd created a Jessica Rabbit-like dress that hugged Suzannah's curves in all the right places and showed just enough leg and cleavage to make his mouth water. But this wasn't a wedding dress, it was a dress woven through with magic. White satin overlaid with silver spiderweb embroidery. Suzannah's hair was done up in a complicated mass of braids covered in netting and silver embroidery, the effect was supernatural. She embodied the spirit of the orb weavers he admired so much in his mother's summer garden. Mysterious, magic, sensual.

"Wow. Just… wow."

She extended her hand, eyes soft and glowing. "Shall we get hitched?"

"This is so much better than Vegas." He took her hand and led her through the screen door. The porch was a riot of white fairy lights. Lanterns hung from the trees in the yard, and the light from the bonfire lent an ethereal glow to the gathering. He brought his thumb and middle finger to his lips and let out a sequence of sharp whistles. Slowly the roar died to a buzz and people closed in on the porch. "First off," he boomed. "Thanks for coming to the first annual Hansen Hollows Halloween party."

A few people clapped, others raised their cups.

"We have a little bit of a surprise for you," he began, pulse suddenly racing. "As you know, not quite five years ago, I met the woman of my dreams. And although it took a while, she finally agreed to spend her life being Mrs. Hansen."

Murmurs raced across the group.

"But just as important…" he bent and picked up Lulah, voice suddenly thick. "This amazing human has also agreed to let me be her daddy forever." Lulah's arms wrapped around his neck as their friends oohed and ahhed and began to cheer as they realized what was happening when Judge Brewer came to stand next to them. "But we all know it takes a village, a community. And we couldn't do this without you. So, if you'll bear witness, we'd like to get married tonight."

The whistles and shouts lasted for a full minute. And holding his baby girl, staring into the eyes of the woman he loved more than his life, they made forever promises and exchanged rings.

"I now pronounce you husband and wife," shouted Judge Brewer.

"Kiss the bride," someone shouted from the back.

Gunnar raised a hand. "Not yet." He handed Lulah to her mother and dug into his pocket. He held up the necklace he'd designed with Suzannah's help. "Lulah-belle, I made forever promises to your mama tonight. To love her always, and to always be her family, and I want to make the same promise to you." He placed the pendant, three interlaced circles studded with tiny diamonds and with a pearl in the center, around her neck. "I promise to be your daddy forever. To always be here for you no matter what. When you're happy and when you're sad. I promise that you and mommy and I will always be a family, and that no matter where life takes us, nothing can break our love for each other." He kissed Lulah on the forehead, then wrapped his arms around both his ladies, and kissed his wife. The cheers of his family and friends couldn't be heard over the symphony of joy in his heart. "It's a Lulah sandwich," his baby girl exclaimed.

THE BEGINNING OF HAPPILY EVER AFTER

I hope you enjoyed Gunnar & Suzannah's story. Download PRAIRIE REDEMPTION to find out what happens when Cody Hansen returns to Prairie and locks more than lips with Carolina Grace.

Two broken hearts...

A career-ending injury from a bull named Damnation has stopped Cody Hansen's life in its tracks and sent him home to Prairie to lick his wounds. Refusing to accept his career is over, he limps into the office of physical therapist Carolina Grace. The sweet girl next door is now all woman, and Cody can't deny his attraction. But nothing—not even love—will deter him from returning to the arena.

Carolina Grace is unlucky in love. Two times she's been left at the altar. Once is a mistake. Twice is a pattern. She really doesn't wanna know what three times would be, so despite the best efforts of Prairie's well-intentioned match-makers, she's locked up her heart and thrown away the key. Until old friend Cody Hansen hobbles into her office. In spite of her good intentions, she can't help but fall straight into his arms—and his bed.

Are they brave enough for one last risk?

Will the third time be the charm for Carolina? Or will Cody's stubbornness cost him everything? Even his life?

Download PRAIRIE REDEMPTION now!!

"Tessa has done it again. Cody and Carolina bring the heat." - Misty

"Once again Tessa Layne hits the Bullseye!!" - Kindle Customer

Get your copy today.

Do you love sneak peeks, book recommendations, and freebie notices? Sign up for my newsletter at www.tessalayne.com/newsletter!!

Find me on Facebook! Come on over to my house- join my ladies only Facebook group - Tessa's House. And hang on to your hat- we might get a little rowdy in there ;)

Meet the Heroes of Resolution Ranch

They've laid their lives on the line before but now they'll have to wear their hearts on their sleeve for the women they love...

Police Chief Travis Kincaid Has Rules....
· Never leave the door unlocked
· Never mix work and pleasure
· And Never, **Never** kiss the object of your affection

Years ago, the former Navy SEAL learned the hard way that breaking the rules only leads to disaster. Since then, he's followed strict rules to stay focused on his career and keep his heart locked away where it won't cloud his judgment.

Too bad the woman he's fallen for was a born rule-breaker.
In spite of her shady past, Travis finds himself bending the rules... repeatedly, for single-mom Elaine Ryder. In the aftermath of Prairie's devastating tornado, Travis must come to a decision about his future. More importantly, he'll have to decide whether breaking the rules one last time will cost him everything he holds dear... or give him his heart's desire.

Download A HERO'S HONOR today

Meet the Roughstock Riders

A brand new steamy contemporary romance series filled with rodeo hotties and the women that bring them to their knees…

~

He's an ex-con. She's the sweet virgin he can never have.

When disgraced bull rider Ty Sloane agreed to take a job as foreman at Falcon Ridge Ranch, he didn't count on having to share his job or his cabin with twenty-one-year-old rising star barrel racer Maybelle Johnson. She tests his patience by day and drives him to distraction by night, but she's off limits—too young and innocent for the likes of an ex-con like him.

As far as Maybelle is concerned, Ty Sloane can go jump in a lake. The cocky bull rider is a thorn in her side, both at the ranch and on the road. But he makes her feel things no man has ever made her feel, and as she learns about his past, she can't help but develop a soft spot for him.

When trouble finds Maybelle on the rodeo circuit, Ty puts it all on the line for the sweet young woman who's captured his heart, even though it may cost him his freedom.

Download RIDE HARD today!

Also by Tessa Layne

Acknowledgments

I'm incredibly grateful to Anne Valburg for all her medical expertise but especially in rural medicine. Many thanks to my friend Nell, and her amazing little daughter who loves Batman and who inspired Lulah. You added so much to this book.

Lastly, I'm so grateful to my writing team – who make my books and words look so good – Kara, Charity, and Amanda. You help make every single one of my books shine.

To Kait Nolan aka Blurb Doctor – thanks for your wit, and your generosity, you have a gift and I'm grateful to be the beneficiary!

And always to Mr. Cowboy and my fierce, sassy daughters. To coin a bad Bryan Adams song – Everything I do, I do for you.